JAN 2 9 2020

W9-BPM-284

The Wild Hunted

FIC
FLYNN

Flynn, Rebecca

The wild hunted

Rebecca Flynn

HUDSON PUBLIC LIBRARY
3 WASHINGTON STREET
HUDSON, MA 01749
ADULT: 978-568-9644
CHILDREN: 978-568-9645
www.hudsonpubliclibrary.com

Black Rose Writing | Texas

© 2019 by Rebecca Flynn
All rights reserved. No part of this book may be reproduced, stored in a retrieval system or transmitted in any form or by any means without the prior written permission of the publishers, except by a reviewer who may quote brief passages in a review to be printed in a newspaper, magazine or journal.

The author grants the final approval for this literary material.

First printing

This is a work of fiction. Names, characters, businesses, places, events, and incidents are either the products of the author's imagination or used in a fictitious manner. Any resemblance to actual persons, living or dead, or actual events is purely coincidental.

ISBN: 978-1-68433-359-2
PUBLISHED BY BLACK ROSE WRITING
www.blackrosewriting.com

Printed in the United States of America
Suggested Retail Price (SRP) $17.95

The Wild Hunted is printed in Calluna

To my baby sister Pamela...

Over the years, you were more supportive than I could've asked of anyone. When I needed input, you always jumped in to be the first to read whatever it was. You were always my greatest supporter. I know you're beside me right now, watching me take this step. I can never thank you enough for being my biggest fan. Gone but never forgotten.

The Wild

Hunted

Prologue

An unmarked delivery truck rumbled to a stop in a dark parking lot behind a shadow-covered building. The driver's door popped open and a large man jumped to the ground. Keys jingled as he landed. He casually walked around to the back of the truck. The smell of diesel mixed with a hint of rain in the night air.

"You're late," a tall, heavy man in a security uniform said from an open doorway a few feet away. "It's twelve after ten. I was told you were supposed to be here no later than a quarter till ten. That's damn near thirty minutes. What the hell took you so long?"

The driver pulled out a pack of cigarettes and a box of matches. "When you gotta go," he said as he put a cigarette between his lips and slid a match from the box. "Can't help that kinda thing." He struck the match and it hissed to life, illuminating his features. He was scruffy at best with dark eyes that almost disappeared as the match burned out.

"Learn how to keep a schedule or we'll be forced to find a new transport company," the man in the doorway responded angrily. "Now get that stuff inside. The curator's been waiting all night."

There was a sharp intake of breath and the delivery man exhaled long and steady. The smoke trailed from his lips.

Inside the museum, Dr. Stephanopoulos paced nervously in a corridor. He could not figure out what to do with his hands. They were in his pockets and then at his sides. They quickly moved to the front of his body where he clasped them tightly. His insides fluttered like a hummingbird's wings. He wiped a bead of sweat from his brow and licked his dry lips.

A young girl sat on a bench in a frilly black dress. Her feet dangled and she happily hummed to herself. She watched her shiny black shoes as they passed over the equally shiny floor.

"How long before we can go to the party, daddy?" the little girl asked.

"Hopefully not long, Eve. We just need to wait for a very important package for daddy's job," the Doctor responded in a heavy Greek accent.

There was a noise down the hall and the sound of footsteps followed. A breath caught in his throat at the sudden noise. When he saw who was there, he let out a sigh and stopped.

The man from the doorway appeared with a small package about the size of a shoebox. "Doctor, your shipment's arrived. Everything's being delivered into the back storage room for logging except the one piece that you requested." He held the box out to the doctor. "I've already signed for the rest of the shipment. They just need you to sign for this piece."

The curator placed the wooden box on the end of the bench where his daughter sat and turned back to the guard. "Just give me the clipboard. I'm already quite late." He grabbed the board and reviewed the items listed. Without a glance from the paper, he said, "Eve, don't touch that."

The young girl looked at the box with curiosity. Something buzzed in her ears and she leaned towards the package. Her head tilted to the side the way a dog does when it hears a high pitched sound. The shiny finish glistened in the artificial light of the museum. Her eyes never left the wooden case. She leaned closer and closer as she reached a tiny hand to touch the item that silently coaxed her near.

Eve's finger barely brushed the handcrafted finish. She immediately pulled her hand back and hopped off the bench. Without a word, she ran down the hall as quickly as her legs would carry her and turned the corner.

Dr. Stephanopoulos turned and reached for the box. He looked back at the security guard. "I trust that your staff has been informed of the importance of how this box is treated? Pandora is not to be trifled with, understood? Nobody is to touch it, open it, carry it around, move it... Let's just say: Nobody is to be in the same room as this item without my presence. Is that clear?" he asked.

The guard nodded and began to turn around. He mumbled something under his breath.

"Do you feel that? It's not supposed to..." the doctor began to say. Goosebumps rippled down his arms. A massive explosion broke the silence and everything in the museum went dark.

Through the dust and debris, Eve took a few steps and breathed in deeply as if she had not taken a breath in thousands of years. She shook her head and said, "Why do humans always think it is actually a box." Her fingers clenched as she stretched her arm straight out in front.

Where the bench once sat, a pile of rubble shifted. The curator's bloodied corpse laid exposed. It twitched. The mangled body slowly pulled itself from the broken walls and ceiling tiles until it stood upright in front of the child.

"Hello, daddy. You may have been the first man to die but there are so many others waiting behind you. From the moment my real daddy gave me my first breath, I began plotting man's last breath. Come, daddy. The inevitable demise of man is upon us. I have many nightmares to release," she said as she took his hand in hers.

With his last breath of humanity, the curator sighed, "Yes, Eve, darling."

She giggled. "Eve, the first woman. How poetic," she said as she skipped alongside her father.

Chapter 1

A cold wind rushed between the buildings of downtown Philadelphia. The early morning fog slowly made its way up the concrete walls. A pink hue crept up into the sky to mark the approach of the morning. The smell of gasoline mixed with the crisp scent of rain. In the distance a few clouds slowly crawled through the dark sky.

Down an alley, Haydeez glanced behind herself before she turned. She ran deeper into the darkness and chuckled. Her heart beat steadily in her chest; her breath was calm. With each stride her blonde ponytail bobbed up and down. "Dawn's coming. You don't have much time," she said. Her eyes sparkled and scanned the shadows for movement. Even in the sudden lack of light her eyes adjusted easily. "Why does everyone always run from me?" she asked.

An iron chain dangled loosely from her hand. Bits of mistletoe were woven into the links. "Come on. I just want to talk."

Haydeez sidestepped just as a tiny hand shot out of a pile of garbage. Her heart skipped a beat. "Trying to trip me?" she asked as she spun around.

A bulbous figure exploded up from the pile and bounced away. It made a path towards the entrance of the alley.

With a flick of her wrist, the iron chain went sailing after the creature. It wrapped around the creature's arm, jerked it to a halt, and dragged it to the ground. A loud screech escaped its puffy lips as it tried to escape the burning pain from the touch of the items. It rolled towards her and trapped itself in the chain.

"Oh please. It's just a bit of Christmas cheer. I know it's early but I was feeling extra festive this year." She casually walked over and knelt down next to the puffy form as it writhed on the ground. "Give it a rest. It doesn't hurt that bad," she added. Her adrenaline pumped but her breathing never changed. As she stood up she said, "And now we go someplace where we can be alone," she smiled a devilish grin. "Shall we? As if you have a choice, right?"

With no effort at all, she lifted the creature and headed towards the entrance of the alley.

The sun had begun to peek over the horizon and quietly slunk into the streets. Haydeez held the creature out into the sunlight and watched. Little by little, it became heavier as the rays of light touched the creature's flesh. It took less than a minute but the creature had turned entirely to stone. The woman tucked the statue under her arm and began to walk away.

A few blocks over she found her Jeep where she had left it. She did a little fake trip and let the statue slip in her fingers. "Oops," she chuckled. "Just kidding." She placed the stone figure into the back seat, careful not to tear her upholstery. She then climbed into the front seat and started the Jeep.

The growl of the engine broke the early morning silence. She pulled out her sunglasses and let her shoulders relax. She shifted the Jeep into gear and left the empty parking lot. "Almost there little guy," Haydeez said with a smile and a glance in the rear view mirror to make sure the stone figure was still there.

The Jeep turned into another empty parking lot. Haydeez made sure to keep the back seat in the sunlight as she drove around an abandoned building. The engine idled for a moment while she looked around. No other vehicles were nearby, no people walked around. She turned off the engine and grabbed a bag from the floor of the front seat. She removed a large flashlight that looked more like a weapon and less like an innocent utility item.

Haydeez hopped out of the Jeep, slung her bag over her shoulder, and grabbed the creature with her empty hand.

In the glow of the early morning sun, her blonde hair shone like gold. Her white tank top and torn jeans covered a naturally tan, muscled body. The chill in the air left goose bumps on her skin where sweat was quickly cooled. She walked tall, as tall as you can in a five feet, five inch frame. Her mission was to capture and interrogate and she was halfway there.

She tucked the flashlight under one arm and pushed her sunglasses onto the top of her head as she walked to the door.

Shadows greeted Haydeez inside the open door of the building. "Fifteen seconds to the back hallway, five seconds to the room, three seconds to the window," she said. "With 22 seconds to spare," she added with a smile. She clicked on the flashlight and took off at a sprint. The door slammed behind her.

Her footfalls were nothing more than a whisper as the soft soles of her moccasins touched down. "Thirteen, fourteen, fifteen," she said under her breath. She turned to her right down another hall and counted again. "Four, five." She turned to her left and kicked the door open. "One," she headed straight to the window.

The creature began to wriggle as it started to turn back to flesh. She stood in front of a curtain and placed the creature on the floor, concern never apparent on her face. The chubby stone creature was positioned to face the corner where Haydeez went to stand.

Yesterday, before dark, she had scouted the building to make sure it had not been in use. She had cleared the floor to ensure there was enough room to work. A single chair sat in the corner where she watched the creature and waited for it to become full flesh again. She leaned on a shoulder against the wall, ankles crossed, flashlight still in hand.

As the creature made its final transformation back to the spongy flesh and blood, she reached over and placed her empty hand on a cord, patient but ready.

A howl of pain reverberated throughout the deserted building.

"Look, if you keep doing that, I'm just going to open those shades," she said as she pulled the cord and a sliver of sunlight slid into the darkness. "Do you want me to turn you to stone and smash you?" she asked as calmly as if the question had been if he wanted cream in his coffee.

The creature tried to bounce away but could not get the leverage it needed with its spindly arms pressed against its body. "No!" it howled in frustration.

"Then this is how we'll do this. You answer me. I like your answers, you stay flesh. I think you're screwing with me, you become bits of gravel in my driveway." She turned off her flashlight, placed it on the chair, then walked over and crouched down close to the creature's face. "Deal?" It looked from the window to the woman and back again several times. Finally, the creature shook its head vigorously.

The woman smiled. "Good boy... um girl. What the hell are you? I can never tell you things apart," she said as she stood up.

"I be everything and nothing. I be both and neither," a gravely Scottish voice answered. He glared at Haydeez, his yellow eyes full of hatred.

"Oh please," she rolled her eyes. "Somebody wants a tan today." She reached back and pulled the cord to open the curtains more. "I can sit here all day and night."

The creature smiled triumphantly. "Ha! Once night falls, you hold no power over me."

She held back her laughter and took a narrow case from the bag. The creature looked confused. When she opened the case, the creature cocked its head to the side. Haydeez removed what looked like a flashlight with an elongated exposed bulb. She raised an eyebrow and with a smirk, she added, "I warned you."

Without another word, she pulled the curtains closed and flicked the switch. A light fluttered inside the bulb. Then, the room was instantly bathed in color. The creature pointed and laughed for a moment until it noticed that its fingers had grown very heavy very quickly. Its body quickly followed suit.

"I be a man! Wait! I be a man!" he shouted.

The light disappeared and a loud sigh echoed through the room followed by a snicker. "So much for 'no power' huh? Now," she flicked on her smaller flashlight. The light bathed her face in an eerie glow as she held it up to her chin like she was getting ready to tell a scary story. "Where do we start?"

The creature breathed heavily and asked, "What be that manner of magic, witch? No mortal wields the power of dawn like that."

"This?" she asked as she picked up the large light. The creature flinched. "Concentrated sunlight in a neat little package. It's a UV bulb times 100. Handy against vampires, shadow creatures, and trow like your funky little self. Keep that in mind, my friend." She gently put down the bulb and sat down on the chair. "Now let's try this again. Where are the babies?"

The trow squirmed. "Hidden safely amongst friends," it answered. "They must be protected. For soon there will be no more."

The woman turned the beam of her flashlight and pointed it directly into the creature's eyes. "Explain. What will be no more? And whose friends are they with? Who do they need to be protected from?"

"Point yer torch away, witch. It hurts me eyes." The trow squinted as he added. "Chaos comes and ye canna stop it. The chalice overflows with evil. Domhan will cease to be."

Haydeez leaned back and reached for the cord. "What are you talking about? What's Domhan? You're about to be pebbles in my shoe if you don't speak clearer." She pulled the cord slightly.

"Wait! I have told ye all that I know!" he shouted. "I was just released and told to play."

She jerked forward, leaned her elbows on her knees. Her heart skipped a few beats. "Released by who? Released from what? Answer me now! You need answers more than I need a new driveway."

An aggravated look crossed the creature's face, as if being turned to stone was preferable to a chat with this woman. "Ye humans have no manners. Me name is Robley, not creature. And I know not who released us. One moment, there was darkness. The next, a gealach so bright it was blinding."

"And you have no idea who let you out or why?" she smacked her hands on her legs. "Well, this was a wasted venture." Her patience began to run out. She had been hired to find out why all those babies had disappeared and so far all she had gotten was this pudgy little legless creature and his circles around the truth. She stood up and clicked off the flashlight. With her empty hand she reached back. "At least I have a new lawn jockey." She smirked again and pulled the cord. The curtains opened to bathe the room in sunlight.

Robley screeched. His body wriggled on the floor, eyes filled with terror. His tiny trow heart jumped into his throat as he screamed, "But you said I would live!"

She leaned down to pack up her bag. "I didn't say I was going to kill you. I want to keep you around. You might remember something later." She zipped up her bag and tossed it over her shoulder. After a quick look at her watch she said, "Thirty seconds."

"You're not human, witch. Who are you?" Robley asked, terrified and angry. His body grew stiffer every second.

The woman sighed and said, "I ask myself that same question every day. I always come back to the same answer." A wicked grin spread across her lips as she said, "I'm Haydeez."

A look of confusion was literally plastered on Robley's face. There it would remain until such time as Haydeez saw fit to turn him back to flesh.

Haydeez allowed the sun a few more moments to ensure that her prize was solid. She then picked up the petrified Robley and raced out of the building back the way she had come.

When she reached the open air again, she spoke out loud to nobody, "Did you get all that, punk?" She tossed her bag into the front seat and gently placed Robley in the back again.

A static voice responded. "Got it." There was a pause. "Why 'punk'? Of all the things you could call me, 'punk' is not top of my list."

"And what would you prefer?" she said as she jumped in the front seat and put on her sunglasses.

"Perhaps a loving term of endearment to show exactly how much you care. You know I'd change my last name to Blackhawk for you when we get married. After all, you love me. You just don't know it yet," the voice responded.

"Well, *darling*," she rolled her eyes as she stressed the word. "Perhaps you could whip me up a little trow containment unit by the time I get there."

The voice laughed. "Was that so hard? And I can whip you up anything you need, baby."

The engine roared to life and a familiar metallic voice sounded. "*Calculating route.*"

"Just the containment unit. I'll be back tomorrow. Think you can handle that?" Haydeez asked.

"I can handle anything you can throw at me."

Haydeez rolled her eyes again. "And you're not even my boyfriend, Linx."

He brushed off her comment and said, "Bebo misses you. He said he likes when I share Twinkies with him."

"Do not feed him junk food!"

"He's a goat, love. He eats anything."

"I will pound you into the ground."

"Promise?"

"Goodbye, Linx."

"*Right turn in 2 miles.*"

"Alright Sheila. Take me home."

Chapter 2

Haydeez walked towards the Jeep after a quick meal at a diner in Ohio. Two men walked past her headed in the opposite direction. One spun around quickly and looked her up and down. The other rolled his eyes and grabbed his friend by the sleeve of his beat-up leather jacket and jerked him in the right direction. "We've got work to do," he said and pulled him towards the diner.

"But did you see her?" the first one said and smacked the other man's hand from his arm.

"Do your hormones ever take a break, man?" the second man asked.

"Do they need to? I'm not dead yet," the first one replied.

Haydeez smiled to herself and swung her hips a little as she walked away. She paused for a moment, looked over her shoulder, and winked at the first man. With a smile that was almost an invitation to follow, she turned back around and continued to walk to the Jeep.

From behind, she could hear the first man say, "Aww, did you see that? I could be... ya know, tonight. But instead I gotta sit here and look at your ugly face."

Haydeez grabbed the roll bar and jumped in the driver's seat. With a pout and a wave she mouthed, "Sorry". Her blood rushed through her veins, goose bumps rippled down her arms like an army standing at attention. She would never do something to jeopardize a mission, especially with her bounty quietly frozen in the back seat. However, the rush she felt when she could elicit a reaction like that from a total stranger was enough to keep the adrenaline pumping. After all, it was just a little innocent flirting. It made her feel wanted again after feeling like a used tissue when her ex-husband left. She slid seductively into her seat and started the ignition. The ever faithful Jeep roared to life. With another smile and a wave she shifted into drive and left a completely dumbfounded man in her dust.

After the diner, the drive home was long and uneventful. Around sunset,

Robley tried to wiggle free and escape. Haydeez response was to pull off the interstate, unpack her light and leave it clicked on in the back seat next to Robley. She could see how her complete calm was a shock to him. He was surprisingly quiet for the rest of the drive.

After a nap at a dirty truck stop, followed by a greasy breakfast, the Jeep sped down US93 home to Challis. Idaho always looked so comforting when she drove home.

Linx had asked her once why she had chosen Idaho.

"Small town, cheap land, and the people don't get scared when you fire a gun on your own property," she responded. "Oh and the mountains! I love the mountains," she quickly added with a smile. Haydeez liked her privacy. In her line of work, it helped to have a lot of land. It kept the questions to a minimum and the neighbors even less than that. She felt a warmth bubble up into her body the closer she was to home. As much as she enjoyed her work, her home was her sanctuary, a flag of normalcy that waved valiantly amidst the war all around. For her, everything else could be shut out when she closed the front doors.

The Jeep turned onto Lime Creek road and headed east. Haydeez had stopped to put the top up before she got this close to the Pahsimeroi Mountains. The late October weather was unusually cold. Little blue lights on the dashboard said 48 degrees and it was still before noon.

"*You have arrived at your destination.*"

"One day, I'll get Linx to program you to say 'Welcome home, Haydeez'," she said as she turned off the main road. She stopped in front of an iron gate and entered a code into a key pad. The gate sat between two eight foot stone walls. Atop each wall sat a large gargoyle, ever watchful, in an eternal vigil. "Hello boys," she said to her guardians. The iron gates creaked open and she drove inside.

A long road lined with trees of every fall color led up to a large house. The road was cobble stone lined with gravel. Behind the line of trees on either side was a large open field with a house sized barn. There were a few horses and a goat sprinkled about as she drove past. "Better get Linx to bring in the kids," she mumbled. Even though the ground was not currently covered in snow, Haydeez insisted that her animals get their exercise and then go straight back to the heated barn. Nobody, even the animals, had to feel uncomfortable or cold.

At the end of the road was a circular driveway. At the center sat an empty fountain with a likeness of an angel as it took flight. Due to the early cold, the fountain had been drained already to avoid damage to the pipes. Trees burst with color outside of the drive way up to the house while closed up irises took over in front of the house. Ivy vines crept up the three stories in a deliberate pattern. A thick oak door was set in the middle framed by symmetrical windows spaced perfectly apart from one another. She had designed each and every detail of the property and made sure that it stayed exactly the way she wanted. Everything had to be just right. When she wanted something a specific way, it happened. People never really liked to say no to her.

Haydeez pulled her Jeep right up to the door and stopped the engine. She then reached into the back and pulled out the statue and the light. A shiver rippled over her as the cold air tickled her warm skin.

As she walked up to the entrance, the oak doors opened as if they welcomed her home with open arms.

A tall man in his mid-twenties stood on the other side of the door. He wore ripped jeans with a Def Leppard shirt. His brown hair sprayed in every direction but the right one. "No kiss? And I opened the door and everything," he said in that familiar British accent.

Haydeez shoved Robley into Linx's arms and said, "Keep this on him until you get him in that containment unit." She put the light on top of Robley and walked further into the house. She did not bother to close the door. "And make sure to bring in the kids. I'm not fond of frostbite on Bebo."

"And a hearty 'hello' to you too," Linx huffed as he closed the front door with his foot and flicked on the light with his chin. He tried to balance the statue and not fall in the process. "This is our little informant I take it. Kinda heavy for his size." He turned and followed Haydeez. "Makes me wish I had 'magical friends' who could give me strength tattoos," he added with a strained laugh.

"Sorry. Guess I'm lucky," Haydeez said. "Besides," she began to whisper. "I don't think my father likes you very much."

"Great, thanks for that. I already had a feeling but thanks for confirming it for me. By the way, you do know that Bebo is a goat, right? He can stay outside in the barn with the horses." he said with a grunt as he continued to try to balance everything. His muscles bunched and strained with the awkwardness and weight of the statue. "Honestly, how did you carry this yourself?"

Haydeez spun around and eyed Linx. With a soft voice, she said, "Bebo is more important to me than you are. You think he should sleep in the barn?" she asked, her head cocked to the side. "I think maybe you should sleep in the barn."

"I'll go get him in a bit," Linx answered quickly.

At the end of the foyer, a large living room opened before them, warm and inviting. An oversized leather sectional surrounded a thick wooden coffee table. Antique pictures hung from the walls. Statues from many different civilizations decorated the room. A fireplace ran the length of the far wall. Everything glowed with a soft yellow tint as the fire flickered.

They stepped down into the living room. With a little hop and a chuckle, Haydeez immediately walked over to the one item that would seem completely out of place to a stranger: a shiny 2005 Harley Davidson Heritage Soft tail Classic. The chrome glistened in the light of the fireplace. The lava red accents glowed as if real lava flowed beneath. She ran her fingertips over the leather and whispered, "Did you miss me?" She kissed the handlebars and smiled inwardly.

"Always the bike" Linx mumbled under his breath.

"The day that you can do for me what this bike does, you'll get the same attention," Haydeez said without looking up.

"I'll do anything for that kind of attention."

Haydeez laughed. "Make my ex-husband cry like a five year old girl and we'll talk. For now, get our little friend downstairs while I order some food."

"Already done. They're on the way," Linx said as he headed for a door on the far side of the room. He held the statue with both hands and had the light rested on top. He had to keep it in place with his chin.

"Such a good little house wife," she said as she smacked him on the rear. "A fire going and lunch on the way. What would I do without you?" she smiled sweetly.

A grunt escaped Linx's lips before he said, "Find someone else. I could list at least 100 guys who'd give their left..." he grunted again as he shouldered the door open. "But you'll be hard pressed to find someone as tech savvy as me. So I guess you're stuck with me, love. I'll see you in a little bit," he called back to her.

The glow disappeared down the stairway as the door closed behind Linx.

Haydeez walked into the bathroom and flicked on the switch. Her reflection gazed back at her as thoughts swirled in her head. After a long drive and too much time to think, Haydeez would take stock of her life just to be sure that she was still where she wanted to be.

Steam began to rise as she pumped some soap from the dispenser. *You know there are others out there that can do what you do. Be normal. Be a girl for once. Do you even see what you look like?* She quietly scrubbed her hands and attempted to scrape away the road dirt as she ignored that tiny spot deep down that still wondered what the hell she was doing with her life.

Over the years, Haydeez had learned that this was her place in the world. She had wanted to be normal. She fought her existence from the day she could speak. Being raised by someone who isn't even family was hard enough. Add to it the fact that he was also a hunter and her childhood was almost non-existent.

Years ago, she took the plunge and ran away from her guardian, Joseph Blackhawk. She told him that she wanted to be just another face in the crowd. In an effort to make herself fit into a mold she found a man that she thought should be right for her and married him. From day one, her heart was not in it. With each moment, she pretended that was where she truly wanted to be. She even gave herself a new identity, since the name *Haydeez* was not exactly common.

Everything seemed perfect. She got to play the cute little housewife to the big fancy executive. Everything she ever wanted was handed to her. Her husband treated her like gold. It was exactly what every little girl that dreamt of being a princess could ever want.

So, she faked her name, her past, and even her emotions for this man until the day her world cracked and fell apart before her jaded eyes. She found out that her husband had cheated on her with not one, but four other women. She felt a combination of relief and anger. Her heart felt freed. Now she was no longer trapped in a loveless relationship but her anger at being deceived was so much stronger. She could not believe that she had been taken for a fool.

So she ran.

Tears streamed down her face as she grabbed only what she needed, left her home in Seattle, and ended up back on the doorstep of her former guardian. Joseph took her by the hand and told her "You are the furthest thing from normal. You're meant for so much more. Being a trophy for some worthless man is not what you will do with your life. You've been used and deceived. Use that anger, frustration, envy, and force it outward into everything you do. Become the best, the most feared hunter the supernatural world has ever met." After a few years in a lie, her heart finally understood what her brain had told her over and over again.

"This is my 'normal'," she said to herself as she gazed in the mirror. One day the final spot in her heart that longed for ordinary things would catch up with the rest of the pieces that were happy with her life.

Haydeez splashed water on her face just as the intercom chimed.

On the screen there was a familiar car with a plastic triangle on the roof that read *Challis Pizza and Subs.*

"Come on up, Bobby," Haydeez said as she pushed a button.

Within moments, there was a knock and the smell of pizza filled the foyer.

"Here you go. The usual: two pizzas, one with everything and one Hawaiian, garlic and cheese twists, a six pack of RC Cola in glass bottles, and of course, one of mom's pumpkin spice rolls. I slipped that one in," Bobby said with a friendly smile.

"You're too good to me. Looking out for me like a brother," Haydeez responded with a smile of her own. She took the food, handed him a fifty, and added "Tell your mom I said 'thanks'."

Bobby pocketed the money and said, "Always do. We just put the meal on your tab." He paused, a look of concentration on his face. He shifted his weight nervously from one foot to the other. "Ma'am, you know that I haven't worked for Challis Pizza in about three years. Anybody can come out and deliver your orders."

Haydeez stared for a moment as if he had spoken another language. "But you're my delivery guy. You always have been. Change is bad. I don't like change," she said.

Bobby smiled. "I'm in college now. I can recommend a really nice guy who can take over for me. They've got a nice guy. He drives a Jeep too. I'd be happy to introduce you to him. I'm sure he'd love to deliver your pizza." He'd tried to get her to understand before but it never seemed to click. He could never tell if she was mentally not capable of handling it or if she was just plain stubborn. He placed bets on the latter.

"Do you have a little brother that can replace you?" she asked.

He shook his head and added, "No, ma'am."

She sighed. "Well then I guess you just have to keep coming out here," she said as she handed him another fifty.

Bobby stood in the doorway, unsure how to respond. He was in his early twenties and had a life of his own. He studied chemistry and planned to move on to get his Masters one day. There were so many things he planned to do in the future and pizza delivery to the eccentric woman on Lime Creek Road for the rest of his life was certainly not one of them. However, he knew when he was beaten and that he would never win this fight. So, he gave up. After another moment of silence, Bobby sighed. "Yes ma'am. I'll see you next time."

"Thanks. Drive careful," she said as she cheerfully closed the door like the conversation had not happened.

As Bobby turned back to his vehicle, he saw Linx with a grey and brown goat on a neon green leash. He waived.

"How's it going, mate?" Linx said as he got closer.

Bobby smiled. "Pretty good. School is rough this semester but I'm making it." He looked down at the ground for a moment and said, "Could I ask you something about Ms. Blackhawk?"

Linx smiled. "Sure."

He shuffled his feet and paused before he asked, "Is there something wrong with her? I mean, not physically of course, but up here." He tapped the side of his head. "I really don't know what to make of her. People talk sometimes and, ya know, I just don't understand."

Linx took a deep breath. "Over the years things haven't exactly been a ride in the clouds. She was abandoned when she was born and raised by the guy that found her. He did the best he could but he's not a replacement for a hug from mum. She tried to find happiness but had her heart broken by the man who said he'd love her forever. With everything she's tried to overcome, she clings to every semblance of normalcy. It's not a matter of control. Once she's happy, changes bring up the pain of her past." He took a long pause and stared off into the distance while Bobby soaked up his words. "Or maybe she's a right crazy bird. My guess is the latter." He turned back with a smile.

Bobby shook his head and walked towards his car. "Thanks, man. That really didn't help me at all."

"It's always good to question things you don't understand," Linx said with a chuckle. "By the way, mate, next time you're wondering about the eccentric behaviors of the lovely Ms. Blackhawk, why don't you look a little further at where that hefty scholarship that fell into your lap actually comes from?" He turned around and walked to the front door.

With his mouth open, the color drained from Bobby's face. The realization that he had never questioned, never even wondered where it had come from, was apparent in his eyes.

With a smirk on his lips, Linx called over his shoulder, "Drive careful, mate." He yanked gently on the leash. "Not that way, you stupid goat."

•   •   •   •   •

"This switches the light from killer sun rays to regular," Linx pointed to a knob that looked almost like a dimmer switch. He reached for a bottle of RC.

"Is that yours?" Haydeez asked, her eyes trained on the containment unit.

Linx cleared his throat. "I was grabbing one for you, love." He froze.

"Right, anyway," she said as she grabbed the bottle from his hand. "Wanna meet our new friend?" she asked as she popped the cap on the bottle. She reached over and turned the dial.

Chapter 3

On a busy street in Chicago, a tall man and a little girl stood on the side of the road and waited for traffic to clear. The girl's black, curly hair was pulled into two perfect pigtails and tied with silver ribbon. She wore a long coat over her black ruffled dress. He wore an expensive suit with no overcoat. She held the man's hand as she patiently watched the cars drive past.

When the cars cleared and the man moved into the street, the little girl hopped happily off the curb and watched as her shiny black shoes smacked the pavement by a pile of snow and slush. With a little giggle, she began to hum to herself as they crossed the road. They headed towards the sound of laughter and Irish music that spilled from the doors of a pub. Other men and women in dark clothing entered the establishment.

A warm gust of air escaped the open doorway followed by the clang of glasses and a toast being made. The man led the little girl inside and they were quickly surrounded by heat as the door closed. A few people glanced at the door but most just ignored the newcomers. Many mourners had come and gone today. Two more did not cause a stir.

The little girl looked around the room. Her eyes stopped on a young man surrounded by a group. A slight twinge in her shoulders told her where she needed to go. She tugged on the man's hand and they walked over to the corner where the quiet group was gathered.

Each man had a glass or bottle in front of him. They all drank as they listened to a single man in black slacks and a charcoal sweater. He had his sleeves pushed up which exposed a brand on his right forearm. His green eyes were one of the only pair that had glanced at the door when the little girl and the man had arrived.

"Excuse me, mister," the soft, melodic voice caused the entire table to turn and look. She smiled and bounced on her toes. "Hello. My name is Eve and this is my daddy." She pointed to the man. "Can we sit with you?"

One of the men reached back and pulled an empty chair over without further thought. The man in the charcoal sweater asked, "What's your business, mister?" He looked up at the man.

"Oh, he can't talk," Eve said cheerfully as she shook her head.

The man closest to Eve looked up at her father and asked "Why?" he cocked his head to the side and added, "He looks a bit ill. His face is all ashen and his eyes look unnatural."

Eve continued to smile. "My daddy is really sick. He's gonna die soon." She looked at the man who had spoken. Her eyes sparkled as she eagerly asked in a childlike sprightly tone, "Would you like to be my new daddy?"

All eyes at the table turned to the little girl in black. The man with the brand spoke. "I think you need to leave now, lassie." He ran his fingers over his trimmed brown hair as he stood up. He crossed his arms and added, "You have no business here."

Her eyes met his. "But I cannot leave yet. I have a gift for you." She sat in the chair as her feet dangled and her hair bobbed to the rhythm. Her daddy stood behind her, motionless, lifeless. "I cannot leave until I give it to you."

With his gaze on her, the man said, "Move along, lads. I'll be done here in a tick." He just stood, eyes on the girl while the men slowly stood, confusion spread across each face.

When the last one left, the man in the sweater spoke. "What is it that you have, little Eve? I'm not a patient man and your words have already caused my defenses to spark."

"I have something you have been looking for, something you thought you could never get back. I want to make you an offer." Eve bounced in her seat.

"Who are you really? The only thing I have been looking for is not something a child could give me. And he certainly doesn't seem to have anything of value," he added as he nodded to her daddy. The man crossed his arms. "Now give me answers or we're done here."

Eve giggled. "I am not a child, silly. This is all I could get when I got here. And *I* am the only one who *can* give you what you desire."

The man cleared his throat. "Enough games, lass. Time for you and daddy to leave." He began to move around the table to escort Eve out of the pub. Without warning, his body was in a chair, unable to move. He shook his head as his brain tried to figure out how he had moved from the side of the table into the chair in less than a heartbeat.

A voice that sounded more intelligent than her years said, "This is not a game, Gavin O'Connell. You may not know exactly who I am but know this:

I am more powerful than you could possibly imagine. I have a proposition for you, Gavin. You are the only one who can accept. If you choose to decline, your other half will remain trapped forever. If you choose to accept, you will be free forever. Free after you have fulfilled your end of our deal of course." She twirled a curl from one of her pigtails.

Gavin eyed the little girl. She knew his name. Anybody could have told her that. He was not married. His 'other half' could only mean one thing and nobody knew about that. She had to be bluffing. The words she used sounded odd coming from a child but he was strangely intrigued. "What do you have?" he asked.

"I have to tell you what I want from you first." Eve giggled again. "There is a man that I cannot find. He is a bad man. He needs to be destroyed but I cannot find him. I want you to find him and destroy him for me. I will give you what you need to find him."

"If you have the means to find this gent, why don't you do it yourself, lass? Seems less involved," Gavin said, skeptical once again.

Eve shook her head. "Oh no; I cannot use it myself. It is special and only one person can use it. You are that person, Gavin," Eve said cheerfully as she clasped her hands in joy. Her eyes sparkled with anticipation, her smile full of eagerness. She was almost bursting at the seams. She wanted to tell him everything all at once.

Gavin sighed. "So who is this bad man and what are you giving me to find him?"

Delighted that he was ready to listen, Eve clapped her hands. "This is the fun part. You have to find the Green Man and destroy him." Her eyes glittered as she spoke. "You are the only one who can do it, Gavin. Your other half has a special connection to him. That is exactly how you will find him."

Gavin tried to hide his surprise. He made it a point not to tell people what he really was. "The Green Man? You want me to kill a legend, a myth?" he asked incredulously. "Everyone knows those are just stories."

Eve snorted. "*Now* who is playing games, silly? You and I both know that the Green Man is real. You used to be his right hand. You knew him better than anyone." Her face grew serious, dark clouds formed behind the sparkle in her eyes. "Then when he was tricked by those nasty people and locked up away from you, you lost everything. You were cursed to walk the earth as a man, to be forever trapped as a human; never to know the feel of the wind against your fur, never to know the wonder of racing after your prey and sinking your teeth into flesh and bone. You were hurt and now, this is your chance to take your revenge."

The air had been knocked from Gavin's lungs. He sat with his eyes wide. "Who are you? Nobody knows any of that." He swept his hand out at the people in the pub. "These people were not even thought of when that happened. Their grandparents' grandparents were not even thought of during that." Sweat began to show on his forehead.

Eve bounced happily in her chair. She bumped her daddy and tiny flecks of skin floated down to the floor as his skin crumbled. "I am Eve remember? My real daddy gave me lots of power. It was very unfair that your other half was viciously ripped from you at the same time the Green Man was trapped and now I want to give it back. Your other half has been angry. It wants to make them pay for trapping him. It wants to make the Green Man pay for not allowing you to do what comes naturally. It talks to me, Gavin. I can hear its rage and feel its desire for revenge. So many need to suffer for what has happened. Welcome it home, Gavin. Welcome the Loup Garou to its rightful place and take back what should have been yours from the start. Let the Alpha of the pack go back to where it belongs."

A gold disk peeked out of the top of Eve's dress. It began to pulse and glow with its own inner light. Eve pulled it out so Gavin could see. Tiny symbols thumped and vibrated around four polished rings. At the center of the ring was a cloudy stone. "This is his sad and lonely prison. It is time to set him free."

Gavin swallowed hard. He touched the bump under his shirt in the middle of his chest. "He's there? It's been so long. Give him to me. Now! Release him!" he shouted.

He had forgotten about the other people in the bar and had not even noticed the fact that none of them batted an eye when he yelled. Nobody heard a word they said.

"You must agree to help me and then I will set him free. He knows you are near. He can feel you and is ready. All you have to do is say yes, Gavin. Will you help me destroy the Green Man?" Eve asked.

"Anything! I will do anything you ask. Release him now! He deserves to be free!" Gavin shouted, his voice full of anguish and hunger. His pupils dilated and his fists clenched. He licked his lips in anticipation.

A wicked grin spread across her lips. She sat completely still. "It is done. We have a pact."

Gavin watched as Eve's petite hands held the glowing disk. His eyes never left her as she turned the dials to match the symbols she needed.

She spoke in hushed tones. He heard her say "elpis" and "pithos" but did not bother trying to understand what she said. The gem in the middle of the disk swirled faster and faster. An eerie red light illuminated the four symbols that had locked the creature in its prison. A soft hum emanated from the disk until finally a wave of heat shot across the table.

The shadow of a creature crept out of the center of the stone. It moved over the table like a hunter stalking its prey. It knew that home was near and freedom was upon it. The heat bubbled out of the crystal behind the creature and rippled over the table. It bled down to the floor and flowed out over the room.

Gavin watched in awe as the shadow slowly moved towards him, his hands gripped the arms of the chair, his knuckles white as snow. He did not know what to expect. After all, he had almost slipped into a coma when the creature was ripped from his being all those years ago.

A moment passed as they just sat and stared at each other, waiting for the other to react. A low growl gurgled up from the shadow and out the creature's mouth. Then, in one fluid motion, the creature sprang forward and melted into Gavin's flesh. He gasped as all that heat slammed him square in the chest. His heart skipped a few beats and the air was trapped in his lungs. It burned him from the inside. Then, he collapsed onto the table.

•　　•　　•　　•　　•

When Gavin opened his eyes, all he saw was wood grain. There was a loud ringing in his ears and a dry spot in his throat. He could feel the warm shadow pace in his stomach. It felt heavy and it felt right.

He smiled to himself. *Home,* the creature rumbled inside his head. *And now we can take care of unfinished business. It will be our turn to rule. When we defeat Cernunnous, we will never have to answer to a master again. Freedom,* it growled with excitement.

Gavin lifted his head. Nobody seemed to notice that he had been face down on the table and the memorial festivities had not ended. Eve and her daddy were gone. He did not know where, nor did he care. The Loup Garou was home. He stood up and began to make his way to the entrance of the pub on shaky legs. The creature caught him and helped him move forward. They worked together to move Gavin's human body in the right direction.

Nobody stopped him, nobody spoke to him. It was as if they did not even notice he was there.

Chapter 4

The last few screams began to fade as Robley turned back to stone.

Haydeez growled. "I still don't know who let him out or where he was trapped. Damn it!" She slammed her fist on the table. The bang echoed through the basement. Her blood pumped hard as the anger took over her body.

Linx reached over and took her hand. He dabbed at a fresh wound as he said, "You really need to calm down. We'll find them and then we can get rid of this little weirdo." He pulled out a piece of gauze and moved to wrap her knuckles. His gentle touch was almost invisible. Had he not spoken, Haydeez would not have even noticed he was there.

But she had noticed. Haydeez jerked her hand away. "And you! What the hell! If you're going to ask questions make them useful!" she yelled.

"What? I asked viable, probing questions."

"Really Linx? You asked him where his balls are and if he ever accidently bounces on them," she growled.

"Oi, if you were a bloke, you'd want to know too." He turned around to make sure the switch was locked in place. When he turned back, he faced a furious gaze. "Look, we'll find them. Don't worry."

Haydeez sighed as the adrenaline began to wear off and let her shoulders drop. "But it's not just about the babies anymore. This thing was let out with other ones just like it. We have no idea what they were in or who let them out. All we know is that there were four others." She groaned. "Now I'm going to have to call them and tell them there are others. So I have to find 4 of these little weird things *and* the babies. What if other creatures were let out too?" She turned to look at Robley, frozen in panic. "What if..." She paused.

"What if what?" Linx asked. "At least you can up your price now. Your fee times five is a pretty decent haul." He moved to look at Haydeez's face.

He turned his gaze to see what caught her eye. "What's wrong?'"

She squinted and cocked her head to the side. "What is that?" She moved closer to the enclosure. "Give me a magnifier," she stuck her hand out.

Linx handed Haydeez a circular glass. She pressed it against the enclosure and looked through it. "Get me the camera." She never took her eyes away for fear that what she saw would disappear. Her heart raced with excitement now. She may have gotten the break she was looking for and she did not want to lose it.

After a couple shots, Haydeez was satisfied that her eyes had not played tricks. She finally found the courage to turn away and smiled at Linx. She held up the camera as she said, "A picture says a thousand words."

"A picture of what?" Linx moved over to the glass to try to find what she had seen.

Haydeez pressed a little button on the camera and began to upload what she'd taken. "I thought it was just a scar at first. His skin was burned with something." She paused as she began to type. "Got it!" she shouted with excitement.

Linx stood in silence as he waited for her to explain herself.

"He was branded. That," Haydeez pointed to a blown up image on the computer screen. "That was burned into him." A sense of accomplishment rushed through her body. She wanted to jump up and down and puff out her chest.

Linx looked at the image. "What is it?"

"I have no idea," she said. "But I am going to find out." She turned to face Linx and smiled innocently. "You want to do some research for me, right?"

Linx groaned. "Don't give me that look." He crossed his arms and she began to bat her eyelashes. His cheeks flushed pink. "That is so unfair."

"Not unfair. I just go with my strength," she laughed. "Thanks Linx. I got some other research to do and I figured it would go faster if we split up the work." She turned and hopped onto the stool in front of a laptop.

"You are so cute when you do that," Linx mumbled under his breath. He walked over to the desktop computer where the image was still pulled up and said, "So what do I get for doing this?"

Haydeez laughed. "You live in my house. I feed you. I get you anything you need. What could you possibly want?" She asked, eyes fixed on her screen as she typed.

Linx snuck up behind her, leaned around her, and kissed her on the cheek. "You don't give me everything I need," he whispered. With a smirk on his face he turned and walked back to the computer.

Haydeez just shook her head and chuckled. "Almost everything then," she said under her breath.

•　　　•　　　•　　　•　　　•

"Does this sound normal to you?" Haydeez asked. She turned on the stool with the laptop and started to read. "Meteorologists are baffled. 'Nobody has seen a storm like that before and we hope to never see one again.' Hold on a sec," she said as she scanned the article for the information she wanted to show Linx. "Here it is. 'Witnesses say the clouds started descending and began to surround the museum and as far out as a block in every direction. One witness claims that she saw the roof explode up in the heavy fog. She also claims to have heard a scream and saw lights flickering.'"

Linx looked confused. "So far it doesn't sound too weird, at least not for what we deal with every day."

Haydeez glanced up and said, "It gets better. 'According to meteorologists, the funnel cloud was inverted.'" She stopped and eyed Linx. "An inverted funnel cloud? What the hell causes an inverted funnel cloud?"

"It would have to be an incredible amount of energy. Hold on," Linx said. He typed into the laptop and a few websites popped up. He turned to face her completely. "When a normal funnel cloud forms," he began. He pointed at the computer screen over his shoulder. "There's electrical energy in the upper atmosphere that causes the tornado to start spinning. This is all in the simplest of terms of course." He clicked one window closed and pulled up the next. "What if there was something really powerful that descended with those clouds." He stood up and started to pace. "Think of an explosion like that one." He pointed to the screen again. "It starts at a central location and then, BOOM..." He threw his hands apart. "It expands outward." Their eyes locked. "And shoots straight up at the same time." He glanced at the computer screen. "With all the power required to create a tornado, whatever did this, it's got to be huge."

"So it was some kind of energy. Energy trails we can track. Any theories? Have you ever heard of anything like this before?" Haydeez asked.

Linx spun around and started to type again. "I've heard of tornados the size of two football fields at the base and ones that travel all over a state but never one that did a backflip and landed on its head. And as far as what could create something like that, aside from Zeus wielding lightning bolts, I don't see a mortal anything that can wield that kind of power. No matches with what we have in the database either. Also, I haven't been able to find anything on that brand. I have no idea where it came from. My guess is that it's some old school, pre-civilization symbol, something from before man." He sighed and rubbed his hand over his chin. "We are definitely going to need some help on this one."

"You think it's a god of some kind?" Haydeez stopped and thought for a moment. "That museum had to have security, right? Why don't you do what you do and get some security footage? I'll see what I can dig up about this symbol. I'm almost certain Lian can clue me in on this."

Linx turned back to the monitor, an eager smile on his face, and began to click away. "Now, security violating, that's what I live for, baby. Give me twenty minutes and I'll have footage from the last year."

"Just the one day, Linx. I don't need the authorities hunting me down for hacking the University of Pennsylvania Museum of Archeology and Anthropology security system," Haydeez said sarcastically.

Linx scoffed. "You underestimate me, like I'd get caught." He laughed and shook his head as he continued to type.

After seven or eight rings, a rushed voice answered. "The Third Eye. How can I help you?"

"Keeglian? Are you alright?" Haydeez asked.

"Haydeez? Is that you, dear?"

"Yea. Is everything ok?"

Keeglian cleared his throat. "Of course, just a very busy time of year. You forget, Halloween is coming and everyone thinks they're a witch around this time." He sighed and then lowered his voice. "What can I do for you, love? You're not out of powder yet are you? I just made a new batch yesterday because I had a bad feeling that you might need it."

"No, I still have plenty. Didn't need it for my latest capture. Apparently, mistletoe and iron work really well on a trow," she said as she glanced at Robley. "I do however need you to take a look at something. I'll have Linx send it right now."

Keeglian sighed. "I hate computers." He paused for a moment. "Watch the front for a moment, dear. I have to step in the back."

A sweet female voice responded. "Yes, sir."

Haydeez could hear footsteps and the creak of an office door. If she had listened closer, she would have also heard a lock click into place. She waited until Keeglian spoke.

A few moments passed with the only sound being the click of a mouse or the keyboard on both ends.

Finally, Keeglian said, "That doesn't look very familiar at all. Do you need an answer right away?" he asked.

"As soon as you know anything, I'd love for you to share. Linx thinks it's pre-civilization but the only things around were animals," Haydeez said as she paced with the phone.

"Not true. While there were animals, there were also gods or angels or whatever your religion dictates." He cleared his throat. Haydeez rolled her eyes and looked at Linx with a tired expression. Her shoulders slumped and she moved her neck. She mouthed *Story time* and continued to pace. Linx had to stifle a laugh before he turned back to the computer screen. With his back to the monitor, all she could see was the occasional shake of his shoulders as he quietly laughed.

"Before humans took their first breaths, demons, devs, angs, gods, dragons, and the fae walked the different planes of existence. It's safe to say that this symbol does not belong to the dragons. They moved on to a different planet long ago. It's been said that they grew tired of sharing their world and one day they just flew up, all at once. They haven't been seen since. Some believe that they settled a new planet and made their home somewhere else in the universe but nobody truly knows where they went but we all have our theories." He paused.

"The ang and dev walked the earth as the gods of animals long before they were elevated to "angel" and "devil" status. That explains why many have features or body parts of animals. Demons walked the earth as well, before the doorway to their plane was sealed of course. This forced them all back into their home. The fae, or elves as you probably know them, went into hiding. As I've met the fae and learned their language, I can tell you that this does not belong to them." He sniffled and muffled a sneeze.

"Gesundheit. What we're trying to figure out is a link between this symbol and an inverted tornado," Haydeez said.

"You might want to take a look at this, Haydeez." Linx stared at the computer monitor.

She turned and walked to the computer. "Hold on a sec, Lian. What is that?"

Linx pointed to an image on the screen. "That would be the little box that caused our 'explosion'. Watch this." He clicked the mouse a few times.

The video on the screen showed a security guard and an older man. They were in the middle of a conversation. The guard handed the man the box.

"Can we get some audio?" Haydeez asked.

"It's gonna take me some time to repair it. Looks like it got damaged during the blast. But this," he paused as he zoomed in. "Check out the box. Professor S is holding something way more dangerous than he realized."

Haydeez watched the screen. "Who is Professor S?"

He crossed his arms and sat back as he continued. "Professor Stephanopoulos, the *former* curator of the museum. He's pretty much at ground zero when that tornado hits," Linx said as he watched the screen, aware of what was about to happen.

Haydeez grabbed Linx by the shoulder, her heart jumped. "What was that? Go back and pause it." She waited. "How far can you zoom in?"

Linx clicked at the keyboard while Haydeez hovered at his side. Her hand still gripped his shoulder tightly.

"Look familiar?" she asked. "Whatever's in that box, that's where Robley was trapped. Get me that audio." She put the receiver back up to her ear. "Sorry, Keeglian. Got anything yet?"

Keeglian sniffled as he rustled pages over the phone. "Too many books. Too many possibilities. What did you find?" he asked absently.

"It's some kind of box with a matching symbol. I'll have Linx clean it up and send it your way," she answered. "Whatever it is, our little trow friend was in it."

Chapter 5

The Loup Garou took a step and felt his legs again for the first time in hundreds of years. He breathed in every scent on the wind. His heartbeat was heightened almost to a point of ecstasy. He stood outside Chicago in a wide open field under a dark sky full of stars but no moon. He looked at his hands and flexed his fingers to help the blood flow freely through his veins. Elongated claws and fur replaced his normally trimmed nails and fair Irish skin. Without the sights and sounds of the city, the creature could feel the pulse of the earth itself. It felt natural and pure. His heart kept pace with the earth's strong, commanding rhythm.

A sigh rippled through his body as he exhaled. He rolled his shoulders and neck. The tension escaped with every pop.

Snow began to fall and the Alpha took a few steps to acclimatize himself to his body. After the nothingness he saw for so long, every sight, sound, and smell was new to him. It was like a child learning to walk or tasting ice cream for the first time. Excitement billowed under his skin so much that his bones threatened to jump out of his flesh.

"It has been too long. Where have you gone brothers? There is much to do," he said to the emptiness of the night. His heart fluttered for a moment. An invisible rope tugged him further north. "You are not as far as I imagined," he said in a slow, deep tone. He took a few more steps and felt the snow crunch beneath his bare feet. "Know that I am coming and be prepared, brothers." He threw back his head and let out a deep, loud howl that carried into the sky and traveled on the wind.

The Alpha cocked his head to the side for a moment. "It will take many days on foot." He growled, angry and disappointed. "It will be quicker by car."

His body began to distort and pop as the beast angrily retreated to allow the human to emerge again. The creature loathed to admit that it had a flaw. While it could travel shorts distances very quickly, it still could not travel as fast as a vehicle could carry it. Anything that could make it feel inferior was usually taken apart at the seams. However, this was one thing that the creature could never destroy. Physical limitations would never go away. Gavin could feel it roar with rage and frustration. He wanted to please the beast. "You've been caged for too long, my friend. Soon enough you will run again and he will suffer for being the cause of your capture," Gavin said to his beast. He spoke as if the creature were a separate entity and not part of himself. They had been apart for so long, it felt like the creature was just a guest in his body.

He turned and walked to a parked car and climbed inside. The engine quietly purred to life. Once again, he touched a bump in the middle of his chest. He felt the warmth and smiled to himself. Gavin began to drive north towards his pack and what he saw as a promising and fruitful future.

• • • • •

"There must be some kind of mistake. He was trapped. We were promised." A tense man spoke in hushed tones to another man as he tapped his fingers on the table. His body shivered as a chill slithered up his spine. "This can't be possible."

"You were the next in line, sir. It only stands to reason that you'd feel it first," the second man said quietly. He leaned forward as he spoke. His eyes darted around the room. "Won't be long now before everyone knows."

A sigh escaped the first man's lips as he stroked his trimmed beard. "No. There has to be another explanation. Get the Doc. I don't care if he's sleeping. Wake him and get him over here, now." He paused. "And remember not to startle the women."

"Of course, sir," the second man said as he jumped up and ran out the door of the tiny café in the small town of White Stag Crossing. Luckily, there were so few people awake at this hour that nobody noticed his wide eyes and the sweat beads on his brow. He wiped his hands down his jeans as he ran.

• • • • •

Thousands of miles away, a bird perched on an ancient tree in a beautiful, lush garden. The bird twitched. The vibrations caused a few leaves to float silently to the ground. A feeling of serenity and happiness floated out and touched every living creature.

Flowers of every color blossomed throughout the garden. A cool breeze from the edge of the grass played in the leaves and tickled the branches. Beyond the grass it was winter, harsher than normal and earlier than usual. Inside these grounds, it was always spring.

The tiny bird chirped a happy song as it looked out over the perfectly trimmed greenery and the sun drenched plants it called its home. Several other birds joined its song, comfortable in the knowledge that this place was safe.

Chapter 6

Haydeez wiped tears from her eyes as she continued to laugh. The phone wobbled on the counter where she had dropped it. Her chest hurt and her stomach cramped as she bent over, hands on her sides.

Between clicks, Linx glanced at Haydeez and asked, "Wanna share the joke? I could use a good laugh."

After one last laugh, Haydeez took a deep breath and chuckled. "Keeglian said the good professor somehow got his lucky hands on *the one and only* Pandora's Box." She chuckled again.

Linx stopped and turned to face Haydeez. "No bloody way. You've got to be kidding me." He chuckled. "*The* Pandora's Box? Keeper of all things evil?" He picked up the phone. "Please tell me I stepped back in time and today's April Fool's Day."

Keeglian cleared his throat. "Linx?" He paused. "Linx, I do not and would not ever joke about Pandora's Box. Yes, it is mythology believed to never have even existed. A legend or fairy tale as some would put it. A bedtime story meant to scare children perhaps. However, Pandora is very much real and I suggest the two of you take this a bit more seriously. You have no idea the dangers..." His voice trailed off.

Linx pulled the phone away from his ear. He mocked Keeglian while the frustrated historian continued his rant.

Haydeez took the phone. "You're serious, aren't you?" She flinched and had to pull the phone quickly from her ear as Keeglian yelled his response. A sigh escaped her lips.

"If she's real, all I need to know is what'll end her, and how do I get my hands on it." The laughter had stopped. She did not want to make Keeglian even more angry. She grabbed a pen and notepad and scribbled while she listened.

After a few minutes of silence Haydeez cleared her throat. "So what you're telling me is there's no way to stop her," Haydeez said matter-of-factly. She threw up her hands in defeat. Frustration seeped into her muscles. "Great! Bring on the Apocalypse. Ragnorok is coming."

Keeglian sighed. "Don't be so melodramatic. You always jump to conclusions. I didn't say you couldn't. I just said that I don't know how yet. At least now you know what won't work. What we need to focus on is how she is going to bring about the destruction of man."

Haydeez and Linx just looked at each other. There was no sound from the receiver for several moments.

A soft beep made the pair jump as if someone had set off a bomb. Haydeez stomach dropped as she looked around the room. She expected to see someone else. Then a strange voice came through the speakers of the computer.

"You must be very careful with that. It's a priceless artifact," the voice crackled.

"I'll call you back, Keeglian," Haydeez said and clicked the end button without waiting for a response.

The voice continued. "I trust that your employees understand the need for the extra security?" There was a pause.

"Can we match this up with the video?" Haydeez asked. Her heart pounded against her ribs.

"Just a sec," Linx said as he clicked a few buttons. "Here we go."

They listened as a thick Greek accent explained to the security guard what was believed to be in the box and why it's never to be opened. The curator was very adamant. He continued to explain where the box would be housed.

When he was done, the security chief agreed and turned to walk away. "Superstitious moron. Can't believe kids stories," he mumbled as he shook his head

The curator ignored him and turned. He gingerly picked up the box, took a step, and paused. With a nervous twinge in his voice, he asked, "Do you feel that? It shouldn't feel like that in here."

"That's when the fog dropped," Linx said. "And then," he paused and waited.

There was a loud boom as the box exploded open and the tornado began to swirl. The video feed was immediately lost.

"Wait! Go back!" Haydeez yelled. "Right there! Pause and zoom in." She pointed. "What is that?"

As the box exploded open, they could see an object inside. It sparkled and shimmered with its own glow.

"There's something inside? I thought everything was released," Linx said. "And since when does all the evil in the world come in a gold disk?" He furrowed his brow in confusion.

"Good question," Haydeez said. "Anything after this?"

Linx continued the video. "Just a lot of snow." The sound of white noise steadily crept from the speakers.

"Ok, can you get me a clear image of that disk? I want to cross-reference it with any other myths about evil or gold disks or anything relating to Pandora. Also can you," Haydeez stopped. Her heartbeat even quieted as she strained to listen. "Do you hear that?" she whispered.

They both leaned forward as a soft voice came through the computer speakers. At first they couldn't make anything out. The voice was too quiet. Slowly, they began to distinguish words.

"Eve, help me. I need help. Will you be my friend and help me?" It was a woman's voice. It had a melodic tone, almost like a pre-school teacher or pediatrician talking to a child. She sounded hurt, sad, and a little alone.

They glanced at each other but neither said a word as the voice continued. "Eve, you came. You are such a special little girl. You are exactly the kind of friend I have needed for so long." She sounded relieved.

A second voice started. It caused chills up their spines and goose bumps over their bodies. "I can't see you. Are you hurt? It's so dark in here. Have you seen my daddy?" The voice sounded young, maybe ten years old. She seemed scared and confused.

"I am fine and he is fine too. And do not worry I can see you. Eve, I need you. Do you think you can help me? Your daddy can come and help too." The woman's voice sounded soothing, relaxed now. It was as if she had waited for someone to come along and find her.

Eve was quiet for a moment. At the mention of her father being there she had perked up a bit. Then she said cautiously, "Ok, if my daddy will be there too, I guess I can help you."

Then there was an eerie sound, almost like a gasp and then a sigh. They both shuddered at the noise.

Then the child spoke again with the intelligence beyond her years. "Hello, daddy. You may have been the first man to die but there are so many others waiting behind you. From the moment my real daddy gave me my first breath, I began plotting man's last breath. Come, daddy. The inevitable demise of man is upon us. I have many nightmares to release."

They heard a ragged breath and the curator's voice say, "Yes, Eve, darling."

The child giggled. "Eve, the first woman. How poetic," she said.

After that there was silence.

"Is that it?" Haydeez asked.

"I don't know. I guess so," Linx said.

"Who the hell is Eve? And why does Pandora need her help?" Haydeez just stood there, lost in thought. She subconsciously held herself and rubbed her arms like she was trying to keep warm.

"And what does she need help with for that matter? I mean, it's Pandora, right? The one who supposedly causes the downfall of men? Why would she need Eve for anything?" he asked incredulously. He shook his head and rubbed his face. "Maybe we should sleep on it. We've been at this for days now," Linx said. He put a hand on Haydeez shoulder and added, "Sleep is good, love. Come on." He tried to guide her out of the room but found his effort to be fruitless. She just stood, eyes focused on something not there.

Linx sighed, shoulders slumped and added, "I know that look. G'night, love."

Chapter 7

As Gavin stood outside the small town of White Stag Crossing, the pack mentality surged through his human body. He could feel every member. Some he recognized and remembered, while others felt new. It made his heart pump faster and the edges of his bones tingle. Every nerve flicked as each member touched him in the back of his mind.

He stood in the snow and inhaled the air all around him. "Females," he growled. "Our pack killed and ate the females and now they are cohabitating. They've grown soft without me." A low rumble escaped his throat. "A mistake that will soon be remedied."

Gavin began to walk into town. The drive had taken a couple days and only because the human in him had to rest so often and he had to drive around the mountains. The creature would have been content to continue or even leave the vehicle behind and make his way directly over the mountains. It despised the human's needs. Everything about the human side disgusted the creature and the sooner it could be rid of him, the better off he would be. He intended to make sure he had to spend as little time as possible as the hairless, fleshy being.

The heart of the pack pulsed with every step. He could feel them gather in the town. The pack, his pack, would be whole again. His heart jumped every step he got closer to them.

A rumble began again in his belly. It called the creature forth. The rumble crept up his chest into his throat. Gavin released a sound that, while normal for the creature, should never be heard coming from a human's lips. His howl vibrated the trees and made the snow drifts shift all around him. It boomed as it passed through the trees and into the town before him.

Gavin smiled a toothy canine grin as he walked into the center of town where his pack had gathered. Over a hundred men and women crouched, visibly shaken but still awaited the orders of their Alpha. He could find them if they tried to run. They were trapped now. Fear bubbled off them like steam off a hot meal.

"My pack. You have grown since last I was free." He sniffed the frozen air again. "And you've muddied our numbers with the filth of females. We are a pack of men. Females taint our strength." He spat as he said the word 'females', yet another thing that disgusted the creature. While he still had the base instincts of the animal, he did not want to admit their usefulness. Even as a human, he never actively sought out the companionship of a woman. While the flesh appealed to him, the idea of a relationship caused him to push away women and remain alone in his bed. He had not yet noticed that there were some females that bowed before him.

As he walked towards the crowd, some of the townspeople who remained on their feet held children, confusion and fear evident on their faces. Gavin could taste their panic as is bubbled and boiled from inside them. The taste was as thick as honey edged with a sweet berry. A tastier snack he had not eaten in a very long time. The pack remained silent as his eyes floated over each face in search of something.

"Where is my second?" Gavin's voice carried over the crowd in the still night air. He scanned the crowd again as he waited for the man's response. The black sky twinkled overhead in anticipation of the morning light soon to come.

A man stood slowly in the middle of the crowd through no will of his own. It was as if he was a marionette and the Alpha was the puppet master who forced him to stand and be recognized. His dark brown hair was trimmed close to his head. In spite of the cold, he wore just a long sleeved t-shirt and a pair of jeans. "We were told you'd been trapped. After all these years, how did you finally escape?" the man asked. He chose his words carefully and wiped his hand nervously over the leg of his jeans. Even in the snow, little sweat drops began to appear above his brow. His bare feet shifted in the snow.

A wicked grin played across Gavin's lips as he said, "I was freed, given a second chance." He spread his arms in a welcoming manner. "Join me, brother. We have work to do, plans to make."

Unable to resist an order from his Alpha, the man stepped over people to get to Gavin. A pained look crossed his eyes as he tried to resist. He knew that everyone here was now doomed. These people had looked to him for protection for all these years and in a matter of a few minutes, he had not only let them down but sealed their fate.

"My Alpha, we haven't 'hunted' in many years. We're a quiet town trying to live our lives, keeping to ourselves. We've made an existence here. Nobody from other cities bother us. Why would you have us leave now?" the second in command asked cautious to not make eye contact. The situation was already dire. There was no reason to make it worse.

Gavin threw his head back and laughed hard. "A life for yourselves? That's so sickeningly human of you. You've grown softer than I thought." His face turned cold. His eyes were like black pools of endless nothing, drawing in victims. "Perhaps I should give you a reason to leave," he growled, a slow, steady warm ripple cascaded from his body. His eyes narrowed as he leaned forward slightly. A heavy vibrato flowed from his lips as he said, "How long will it be before the nearby town questions how you stay so young? How long do believe you can stay hidden in these mountains? You think they don't see you? You think they aren't watching? There's a reason they don't come here, brother. There's a reason they don't ask. I can feel the clouds of fear, even this far away. Humans fear what they don't understand, brother. Perhaps we should help them understand and give them a reason to fear." He leaned a little closer, his breath almost directly in the other man's face. He whispered, "Whether by my will or necessity you will hunt again."

The pop of bones filled the crisp air as he began his change. He threw his head back and pushed the creature to the surface. The other man took a few steps back. The beast stood before the pack in a matter of seconds. His almost eight foot tall frame pulsed with a heavy, hot energy that sent vibrations out to his subordinates.

One by one, each cowering pack member began the change as well. The creature's warmth flowed over them like a tidal wave. It took them down five or ten at a time. The weakest members were the first to turn. Most of them were new pack, born into the change. They were low on the food chain and could not resist the Call. Large dogs of many different colors replaced the humans in the Canadian snow.

The Loup Garou watched as the last of his pack turned, his second being the final change. The man had collapsed to the ground in one last feeble attempt to resist but had failed like all the others. The creature breathed in their scents once more. He paused and cocked his head to the side as an unusual sensation flooded his senses. The normal feeling of pack was there but alongside it flowed another more delicate ribbon of warmth. An eerie smile formed on his canine face. "Female pack. How interesting," he said and slowly scanned the bodies. "You're mine now. My pack. And now we must do what we've always done. We shall see if you're as good as the men." He crouched down and a low growl began in the pit of his stomach, rolled up his throat, and exploded out of his mouth. He looked at the human women and children frozen in horror. Panic overflowed from them, but there was no escape. They stood there, paralyzed, and watched their kin turn to face them. He threw his head back and released a howl that raised goose bumps over the human's flesh.

The winds around the city began to pick up as a chorus of forced howls responded. The initial light of the new day crept up over the mountains as the first screams pierced the early morning air. The wild hunt was on.

Chapter 8

After the fourth day of nothing, tempers burned hot. Linx picked up a broom and dust pan for the third time today and headed to a small pile of broken glass.

"At least you finished the coffee first this time," he mumbled as he bent to clean up the mess.

"What's your problem?" Haydeez snapped.

Linx cleared his throat. "Nothing, just trying to think things through right now."

"Well, I'm thinking that won't help considering you've been about useless so far." Haydeez said, a nasty bite in her voice. She moved to a computer, sat down, and attempted to search for something. Her fingers clicked harder than they should on the keys. Part of her held the hope that something would just pop up and say 'Right here!' She sighed as she had to make a conscious effort not to pound the keys.

With a full dustpan in hand, Linx walked to the stairs and headed up.

"Good, I don't need your help," Haydeez said, her words dripped with anger.

Linx paused for a moment, his heart dropped into his stomach. He sighed and continued on his way. "It's the frustration talking. It'll go away." He mumbled as he walked away. "I'll give it a few minutes and when I come back," he opened the door. "She'll be just as pissed but at least I will be out of the line of fire." He laughed to himself. The moment he left the basement, he could feel the tension lift. It was like walking into an air conditioned building on a very hot day.

After he dumped the remnants of coffee cup number three, Linx went to the fridge to make lunch. Maybe food would calm her down a bit, but he doubted it.

His muscles stopped their irritated dance as he put the sandwiches and some fresh fruit on a tray. Since more caffeine would not be the best idea, he shook his head and replaced the RC bottles with cold water. "Plastic," he said with a grin.

•   •   •   •   •

Linx sighed and rolled his eyes. "I could see searching through all of the ones in Philadelphia, which I already did. Hell, I'll even look through the entire state. It would probably take a bloody year and we'd probably find something somewhere else before I'm done but I would do it. But the entire country? Haydeez, love. That would take an army of eyes that I don't control. Do you have any idea how many traffic cameras there are in the country?"

Haydeez tilted her head back and let out a groan that sounded more like a yell. "All we know is who Eve is. That's it. We need more. I'm not about to sit here with my finger up my nose and wait for something to just 'happen' to pop up."

Linx sighed again. He could feel the knot at the base of his skull start to tighten. "I've got my programs monitoring the Amber alerts. She was, is, a high profile missing child. Don't you think that someone wants that reward for finding her? What we should do right now is take stock of everything we know and look more closely at everything Pandora said." He carefully led Haydeez to the plush couch on the far side of the room and grabbed a pen and notepad along the way.

After what seemed like hours Haydeez lifted her pen and said, "Wait, she said 'I need you'. What if Pandora herself was trapped in the box and needed a willing host?" Haydeez said as she took a bite of her sandwich. "Maybe her spirit can't do what it needs to do without a host."

Linx scribbled a few words and added, "If she needs a host, then so do the creatures. What if Robley is just some poor bum that agreed to do her bidding? That means she needs help completing her task of bringing about the destruction of mankind."

"Meaning?"

"Meaning she has to find willing parties. While that sounds simple, she still needs to find them." He turned to face Haydeez. He saw a light at the end of the tunnel. "Which gives us time to catch up." He wrote something else. "Right, so what do we know about Eve?"

They both paused for a moment.

"Not much," Haydeez said. "She's the former curator's daughter. She's ten years old. We know what she looks like." She paused again. "The only thing I can think of is that Eve just happened to be the unlucky female body close by when Pandora busted out." She shook off a chill as she took a drink. "So according to Greek legend, Pandora was created to destroy man. Then, why would she need a little girl to..." She stopped, a light of excitement in her eyes. "The curator moved here from Greece. Eve was Greek." She jumped up. "What if her host has to be of the same heritage?"

Linx looked up. "So you're saying that whoever she lets out has to be of the same nationality as the unfortunate sod it takes over."

"Exactly!" Haydeez began to pace. Her blood pumped and her brain sparked. "Think about it. Your heritage dictates your beliefs, at least in most cases. Typically, if your blood says Greek, your brain is more likely to be open to the idea of Zeus and Hephaestus collaborating and creating the first female."

From across the room, a tiny beep could be heard. Haydeez and Linx turned. Linx's computer beeped a few more times and then a window popped up. They looked at each other before they ran to the monitor.

"What kind of hit was that?" Haydeez asked as she looked over Linx's shoulder.

"Looks like more than one," he said. She was so close he could smell the soap she had used in the shower last night. His body tingled but he pushed it aside for the moment.

A soft beep continued as they checked the first hit.

"An anonymous tip led to an investigation in the Chicago area. A minor child matching the description of the missing child, Eve Stephanopoulos, was seen with a man matching the description of her father, Dr. Pinuto Stephanopoulos. The Amber alert has been removed as we have been able to verify that this was indeed the missing child, Eve Stephanopoulos." Linx read the Amber bulletin twice. "Well, she did promise Eve that her dad could go too."

Haydeez looked confused as her brain worked overtime and tried to put everything together. Some of the pieces fit but others were just those weird shapes that you can never find the mate for until the very end. "What's in Chicago?"

"Not sure, but I've got another bulletin," Linx said as he moved the Amber alert aside and pulled up the next window, eager to see what else they uncovered. "I had this one tracking weather patterns. I thought this might be useful since Pandora's entrance was in the middle of an inverted tornado."

They both looked at the article. It talked about Canadian snow storms. Although Canada is no stranger to snow, a snow *hurricane* is not something that is seen every day.

"A snow 'hurricane'? That's impossible." Haydeez said as she read further. "And it didn't move anywhere. It started and stopped in the same area. How is that even possible?"

Linx lifted an eyebrow and scoffed. "Really, love?" He looked at the screen and started to type. "Someone who has a Celtic mythological creature trapped in her basement, someone who is trying to track down *the* Pandora and use magically enhanced weapons to stop her from destroying mankind, and someone who has Native American mystical tattoos on her body is saying something is impossible! Right, a snow hurricane in Canada is completely impossible," he said as he shook his head.

Haydeez shoved Linx. "Yea, thanks, point taken. Now save all that stuff. I'm taking a little trip."

Linx cleared his throat. "I think not. You'll not be travelling alone." He turned to face her and crossed his arms.

"Oh really? And who is going to take care of Bebo and the horses? By the way, go bring them in. It's getting a little too cold for my little Bebo to be outside. He gets mad when he gets cold." She crossed her arms in response.

Linx just looked at her and didn't move.

"Fine. Bring the animals in and I'll call someone," she said.

Linx victoriously slid off his stool and said, "Why don't you ask that Bobby kid?"

With a raised eyebrow, Haydeez said, "He delivers my pizza. He's not a babysitter. Find the number for the nanny service."

"Honestly, who calls a nanny for a goat?" He asked. "Oh wait... I just got that."

•   •   •   •   •

"I told you to stop talking. Maybe next time you'll listen." Linx and Haydeez walked out the front door of a pub in Chicago. They left the warmth and were met with an icy breeze that bit through their clothing and attacked the skin beneath.

"Maybe I wanted answers and your 'tip-toe around the bad guys' approach wasn't working."

"You don't understand these blokes. You need to talk like you're one of them," Linx said. "Strong arm doesn't work with them, love." He lowered his voice as the door closed behind them. "IRA boys aren't afraid to die to keep a secret. I've dealt with them before and trust me, you can't win with muscle.

They're just not afraid."

They walked in silence for a few moments. The wind picked up and Haydeez pulled the hood up on her jacket.

The pair turned a corner and Haydeez finally spoke. "At least we know they were here. Where they went after this, I have no clue but they were here and that's a start." She stuffed her hands in her pockets and added, "You can always check the traffic cams and any video feeds from this street the day they were spotted. She doesn't seem like the type to stick around but we might get lucky and at least see her getting into a cab or going into another building or something."

Linx nodded. "Let's just get back to the plane. I don't think I could get my fingers to cooperate right now. I'll check for all that while we're on our way to our next, even colder, location." He shivered. He could feel the air cutting through his coat and clawing its way to his skin.

Haydeez laughed. "You know that I'm supposed to be the girl, right? I'm supposed to be cold all the time and complain because my fingers are frozen and all that."

"Shut up. I can't help that I'm more sensitive to the elements than you," Linx said as he continued to walk with his shoulders hunched and his arms pulled up across his chest.

"Sensitive? You mean you're a big baby when the temperature drops below 70. Come on, breathe in that fresh crisp air." She took a deep breath. "Ok, maybe just crisp and not so fresh." She coughed a little and cleared her throat.

They walked in silence for a few more moments.

A small smile crept across Haydeez's lips. Her shoulders shook slightly as she quietly asked, "Would you like my jacket?" She had to consciously try to hold back a laugh. Her chest hurt from the strain.

"I really do hate you. Really," Linx said as he started to walk faster to get his blood flowing to bring a bit of warmth to his feet.

Haydeez laughed harder as they reached the rental car. They did not say anything else the entire ride to the air strip.

•   •   •   •   •

The click of a keyboard was the only sound inside the cabin of the private plane. Haydeez sat in a plush leather chair bolted to the floor in front of a table. She looked out the window and watched as the clouds floated past.

She always wondered what it would be like to just jump out the plane and flop down on a big pile of fluffy white clouds. Fortunately, she also knew better than to just jump out of a plane like that. *Clouds don't have a floor,* her guardian told her when she was little. *They're not solid like the earth,* he would tell her all the time. *You must always remember to keep your feet solid and let only your soul play in the clouds.*

Linx sat across from her in a matching chair. His fingers clicked away on the laptop in front of him. He glanced up every now and then to make sure Haydeez was alright. He knew how she got when an investigation started to dry up and they had to start all over again. He also knew how she got when she had to fly.

As long as she stayed awake, she would be fine. A headache would creep up on her or she would start to get a muscle spasm between her shoulder blades but once she closed her eyes, that is when the bad stuff happened. She could never figure it out. If she slept on a plane, it was like her brain went into freak-out mode and started with the nightmares. The longer she stayed asleep the worse they got and the more real they felt.

Most people would figure out after a little while that their dreams were not real and the next dream would start. Unfortunately for her, this little reprieve never occurred. She would get further and further into the dream and believe it was really happening. Keeglian had told her that she may end up stuck one day if she was not careful.

So now, whenever she flies, she suffers through the headaches to make sure that she never succumbs to the evils that her brain produces.

Linx continued to search the traffic cameras. He cocked his head to the side and hit a few keys quickly. "You don't literally disappear when you turn a corner right? I mean, I know the turn of phrase 'He disappeared around a corner' but unless I'm mistaken, that doesn't actually happen." With a raised eyebrow, he turned the computer and said, "Take a look."

Haydeez turned to look at the screen and clicked the play button. "That's our girl," she said as she watched.

Pandora and Eve's father walked down a street and turned a corner into an alley.

"Ok, so how did they 'literally disappear'?" she asked.

Linx smiled elatedly. He got excited when he could do something better than Haydeez. It was hard for him to keep up sometimes and if he could see or do something first, well, it made him feel like he truly did need to be there. "You didn't see it. I'm better than I thought." He grabbed the laptop and turned it back to face him. As he clicked a few buttons, Haydeez rolled her eyes. He turned it back to face her and said, "Watch again."

She looked at the screen and clicked a few buttons. The view had been zoomed in and cleaned up to street level. She watched for a few seconds. Her nose scrunched up and her eyebrow raised. "She just poofed. She didn't even wait until she was completely into the alley."

The video showed Pandora as she rounded the corner after Professor Stephanopoulos. To an untrained eye, the slight inconsistency would never be noticed. However, to the eyes of Linx, every detail was important. Her right heel was still in sight. It never left the pavement as if she had taken a step. However, in less than a second it was gone. There was no glitch in the tape or a cut that would imply someone had looped it. Pandora had just disappeared.

"So we know she can play Houdini. Now what?" Linx asked.

Haydeez sighed. "Now we check out the snow hurricane."

●　　　●　　　●　　　●　　　●

Fresh snow covered the ground and shimmered in the midday sunshine. Empty houses and small businesses sat silently and watched as strangers prowled the streets of the tiny town. It looked like an old western town with modern touches. A frozen fountain sat in the town square, its statue lightly dusted with new powder. The eyes of the statue also watched the strangers search through its town. There was an eerie sense of calm heavy in the streets. There should have been people, pets, or even wild animals here. But there was nothing.

Haydeez took a few steps and caught herself before she tripped over something sticking up in the snow. She leaned down with a gloved hand and lifted up a bare hand. As she stood up, part of an arm followed but the rest of the body did not. "Not just a storm." She lifted the hand to show Linx. "Something ate these people. An entire town doesn't just disappear like this." Little puffs of white escaped her lips as she spoke.

Linx walked up behind her and said, "Could've been something after the storm. Carnivores, especially in this region, tend to scavenge after a bad storm. They don't come this close to a town just for the fun of it." He took the hand from her. "Yea, those would be bite marks." He took a closer look. "Bigger than I've seen before. What makes a mark that size?"

"I don't think it happened after. I haven't seen any footprints either."

They continued to look around the town without a word. Haydeez stopped, a look of concentration on her face. "Do you hear that?"

Linx looked up. "Hear what?"

"Exactly. No wind, no birds, no trees creaking, no twigs snapping, nothing. I don't hear the sound of snow crunching or animals in the distance. Everything here is dead. Who lived here? And why were they completely wiped out?" A strange feeling of being watched passed over her and she shivered slightly.

After a few steps, her eyes caught sight of the fountain. A tall figure stood in the middle of a large pool of frozen water. Ice crystals covered the erect penis. Long antlers like those of a large stag sprouted from the statue's head. Ivy wove itself around the points of the antlers. His outstretched arms were covered in leaves carved out of the same stone. In his left hand, a stone serpent with horns hung. In his right, he held a staff similar to that of a king's scepter.

Haydeez was mesmerized by the statue. It emanated power and authority. The eyes held an understanding that an inanimate object should not have. She understood where the feeling was coming from now. The figure looked down at her, judged her motives and the reason she trespassed in this village.

"Gives new meaning to 'rock hard', ay." Linx walked up behind Haydeez and looked up at the statue. "Found something kind of strange," he added as he handed something to Haydeez.

She found it difficult to pull her gaze from the statue's face. When she finally looked to see what Linx had handed her, a confused expression replaced the awe she felt from a moment ago. "What is this?"

"Found it on the door of one of the homes. Doesn't look like any kind of wood I've ever seen. And it's warm, almost like it's alive. Pretty weird, ay." He took another look at the statue. "A snake *and* a scepter? Looks like someone's compensating, if you ask me."

Haydeez ignored Linx and held the sculpted piece of wood in the palm of her hand. It was shaped like a bird. Linx was correct. It felt warm, like life flowed beneath the surface. She could feel it even through her thick gloves. The detail was amazing, similar to the statue of the man. She turned it over in her hand to examine every inch. The wood was smooth, no chips or splinters. It looked polished. Someone had taken a great deal of time and care in creating this. It began to pulse in her hand.

"Which door did this come off of, Linx?"

He took some photos of the statue to be able to look it up once they got back to the plane. "The one over there." He pointed to a building that looked just like the others except it had a set of antlers above the door.

She smacked him in the back of the head. "That's not a house. That's a temple." She walked over to the temple and opened the door.

Inside was small. There was enough room for a few small families, maybe ten or fifteen people at the most. It took about twelve steps to cross to the front where another statue stood. At the feet of the statue was a pile of empty baskets. The statue matched the one in the middle of the fountain. On the wall behind the statue was a mural. Someone had painted a huge tree with branches that mimicked the position of the statue. In the tree sat three birds: an eagle near the top, an owl in the middle, and a blackbird where the statue's shoulder would be. Next to the tree stood a stag, tall and proud. Along the side of the tree flowed a river. Above the river, a salmon had leapt up in the air and was forever preserved in the painting. Behind the tree, in the distance stood a pack of dogs.

"What an odd painting for a temple," she said to herself. She pulled out a second camera and began to snap some pictures. "Shouldn't be hard to figure out who you are. Whoever painted your scenery was very descriptive. Lots of detail." She spoke to the statue. She was sure to include the empty baskets as that seemed very odd to her. This whole place felt off. Obviously there were people that lived here because the houses were not in disrepair but the lack of offerings and the fact that no sound could be heard within the town made Haydeez feel more uncomfortable than anything. Her entire body was on edge and ready for an attack.

Chapter 9

A beep sounded as Haydeez and Linx stepped back onto the plane.

"I wonder how long it's been doing that," Linx said as he sat down in front of the laptop. He pulled the card from his camera and inserted it into the laptop while he pulled up the window that flashed. "Well, well, lots of weird things going on around the country. Seems we have a pack of wolves taking over a cargo ship." He started to upload the images from his camera. "Pardon me, it says 'werewolves'. Right, I really hope that's not the only weird news hit we got. If it is, that's sad."

Haydeez sat down in front of another laptop and pulled her camera card. "Never discount information, Linx. It might be important for something later."

They uploaded the pictures and began to search for anything to explain what they just saw.

It did not take long to figure out who the statue was.

"Cernunnous? What is a statue of a Celtic god doing in the middle of a small Canadian village?" Haydeez asked.

Linx laughed. "Celtic, huh? Well, everything just comes together eventually. That little village was the Canadian equivalent to the Amish. It's a self-contained village without the influences of the outside world. Sound familiar?" He glanced at Haydeez. "Not too much is known about the village other than the name and when it was established. Our little town is called *White Stag Crossing*. It looks like it was established several hundred years ago by immigrants from the British Isles." He stopped and looked at Haydeez, an expression of disbelief plastered on his face. "Really, could it be this easy now? It's almost like someone just handed all this stuff to us."

It was her turn to laugh. "Don't get upset when you're given a gift. Sometimes it just happens that way. So, we know the people came from the British Isles and they established a town that worships Cernunnous." She stopped. "The baskets in front of the painting. He's the Celtic fertility god.

The baskets were for offerings. But why were they empty?" she asked herself. "What if they didn't have anything to offer? They looked like they had been empty for more than a week, like they were offered empty," she said as she sent the information they had found to Keeglian.

In a matter of moments, there was a knock and Haydeez jumped a little.

"I hate when he does that," Haydeez sighed and rolled her eyes. "His little 'travel through any door' trick is never going to stop being weird." She stood up and walked to what looked like a closet. With her finger she drew a symbol on the door, knocked twice, mumbled a few words, and opened the door.

A creature walked through the door. It had the legs of a satyr, with hooves and fur. Its head and chest were those of a goblin. Tiny curved horns, about the thickness of an adult male thumb, adorned its dog-like head. "Do you have any idea what you've gotten yourself into today, ducky?" Keeglian adjusted his vest and brushed off his pants. A gold pocket watch was placed gently into his vest pocket. "It surprises me each time I hear from you that you're actually still breathing." He cleared his throat and walked into the room.

"It really creeps me out that you actually look like that," Linx said under his breath without a glance at the shopkeeper.

Keeglian cleared his throat. "Yes, well, as I was saying, you may have finally gotten yourself mixed up in something out of your league."

Haydeez laughed. "Unless you're here to help, you might as well go back through that door. Whatever is happening needs to end. If I just leave it alone, Pandora will have nothing standing in her way."

Keeglian tapped a hoof as he thought. "Alright then, perhaps we should come up with a plan. You do of course, know what happened to that village?" he asked.

Linx and Haydeez looked at each other and shrugged. "That's what we're trying to figure out right now," Haydeez said.

A sigh escaped Keeglian's canine jaws. "The reason that those people worship the god of fertility is because they are his pack. I'd heard that they moved away from their homeland but I had no idea that they were this close to us. Do you know the story of Cernunnous?" They shook their heads. "Of course not. Why would you know anything about history," Keeglian said, irritation in his voice, as he began to pace. His hooves clicked on the floor.

"Not only is Cernunnous the god of fertility, he's also called the Master of the Wild Hunt. He and his pack would pass through towns and destroy every man, woman, and child that he couldn't use. They would come in the night and destroy whole villages. Cernunnous picked the most valuable men of the village and added them to his pack, willingly or not. From that moment on, they would be forced to follow his rule but they would also receive benefits of being his pack. Nothing could destroy them." He turned. "Cernunnous was most active in the winter months. In case you hadn't noticed, this year has been unusually cold. It's almost as if the early winter has helped to fuel them. The pack has been quiet for so long I thought they'd disappeared for good. For some reason they've become active again." He paused.

"Many hundreds of years ago, there was a war waged on the gods of the world. It lasted for over one hundred years due to the nature of the battle. Christianity and its 'higher powers' decided that, in order to bring more followers to them, they had to discredit the gods of the other religions. The only way to do that was to cut them off from their followers, essentially causing a break in their power source. If they could sever the link and prevent the gods from granting gifts to their followers, they could prove that the other gods were just children's stories.

"For years, they tracked the gods of all major religions from Greek and Roman to Mayan and Celtic. When one was located, a task force was sent out to 'handle' the issue. They would trap the gods and goddesses to prevent them from hearing the cries of their true believers. Without the faith of the worshipers, they had no real power anymore."

Haydeez shook her head as she tried to make sense of Keeglian's story. "So what does all this mean now? Was he released or something?"

Keeglian stopped for a moment to think. "No, I believe he is still trapped. This does not feel like the Horned god. He was always said to be cleaner, less wasteful. I don't believe he's behind this massacre. And besides that, why would his followers leave empty baskets for him? To me that says they've tried to continue the vigil but the early winter has destroyed their crops and they no longer have anything to offer. No, he's hidden somewhere and you'll need to find him."

"I'm sorry. What?" Linx said as he leaned forward in surprise. "And why would we do that?"

The roll of Keeglian's eyes looked odd in the head of a canine. "Because, you injudicious creature, you'll have to awaken him to take back control of his pack. Something has control of his dogs and whatever they're doing is most definitely not in the interest of the Green Man."

"Dogs. Hold on. That story you found, Linx, I told you it could be important. Never exclude anything weird," Haydeez said with a smile. She turned back to look at the laptop. "Where were they going again?"

Linx pulled up the story again. "It says the ship was headed across the ocean to the British Isles." He looked up. There was a slight twinge in the back of his mind. "Maybe they're headed home now."

"It's quite possible but why would they do that? If most of the members were forced into running with him and then fled the country when he was trapped, why would they willingly go back there?" Haydeez asked. "It just doesn't make sense."

"Unless they're going back *un*willingly," Linx said.

Silence filled the cabin of the plane. Nobody spoke for what seemed like hours but in reality was only about ten minutes.

"So we have to release this god and we have no idea where he is or what he's trapped in and even if we knew what he was trapped in, we don't know how to get him out. Then, we have to deal with something that's controlling his immortal band of indestructible dogs, again, which is something we know nothing about. Which means that whatever is controlling them is most likely indestructible and immortal as well." He paused. "Great! Let's get moving then," Linx said.

"Your sarcasm is less than necessary," Keeglian scoffed.

"Wait, the piece of wood I gave you, the bird from that door, can I see that again please, love?" Linx reached out a hand.

Haydeez pulled the piece of wood out of a pocket and handed it to Linx.

He held it up and looked at the screen. "Damn, I was hoping I was wrong." He shuddered. With a sigh he mumbled to himself, "Same wood, same detail. Why did it have to be the same?"

Haydeez looked confused. "What are you babbling about?"

"This isn't the only bird like this. I've seen another one similar to this," he said as he wiped his face in frustration. The twinge became a steady pulse. He knew where they were headed next. "Not the same kind of bird but the same type of wood with the same amount of detail." He groaned. "I'm willing to bet that this little bird is how we release Cernunnous." He leaned back in his chair and put his arm over his eyes.

Haydeez and Keeglian eyed each other. "Ok I'll bite. Where have you seen another bird like this?" Haydeez asked.

There was silence again as Linx tried to decide how to answer.

"Let's just say I know someone who has something just like this. It's a different kind of bird, something like an eagle with its wings spread out or something. I can't remember exactly considering it's been a bit since I've seen it but I know it's still there." He refused to meet either of them in the eye.

"Ok then, I guess that's all we're getting out of him," Haydeez said. "Now that we know where they're headed, all we have to do is hope that we can find where Cernunnous is trapped so we can release him. Shouldn't be too hard, right?" She rolled her eyes. Her muscles were already sore at the thought of a flight across the ocean. "So where does this person keep the bird, Linx? We have to get it if we intend on keeping these dogs from slowly taking over villages again." She paused. "Keeglian, these dogs are somehow linked to their master, same as any wolf pack. What if *they* knew how to find him?"

"If they are headed there now, we have to stop them. Whoever is controlling them may mean the god harm," Keeglian said. "I'll see if I can locate any other pieces like your little bird. Luck to you, ducky. I know I can't stop you." Before she could respond, he walked to the open door, stepped through, and disappeared.

Chapter 10

An uncomfortable awkward voice broke the silence. "My Alpha, we're approaching port."

Gavin turned from his meal and said, "It's about time. We've been in this metal bucket for a week now." He growled. "Everyone remains below deck until I say otherwise. No exceptions." He turned back to his meal.

The man spoke with a shudder in his voice. "Yes, Alpha. I'll advise your second and pass the word to the rest of the pack." With a nervous glance at the almost raw meat on the table, the man left. He could not tell what was on the plate and he did not really want to know either. For the sake of his stomach, he closed the door and cleared his throat before he left to find the Alpha's second in command.

•　　•　　•　　•　　•

As the last screams of the local port authority faded into the night, the pack made their way down the gangplank onto the now empty dock. The newer members looked like prisoners walking their last mile, heads hung low with their eyes on their feet. The majority of the females and the men that had not been part of the pack long looked in the other direction when they passed the remains of the man. Those who had been pack members longer looked at the remnants in apology. This was wrong. It was not the pack way.

"Alpha, with all the respect deserved, was that an absolute necessity at this point? If we leave a trail, we'll be caught. Should we be putting the pack at risk like that?" the Alpha's second in command, Kal, asked. He tried to choose words that would not draw anger. His gaze moved between the bloody pile and his leader.

Without any movement, Gavin said, "Do you not believe that our puppies can handle themselves? Our numbers are great enough that we can and will outlast any attack. Don't worry, brother. Have faith in your pack." He crossed his arms and watched patiently as the last of the people left the ship. "And now we move. It'll take time to get to our destination." The Loup Garou paced inside Gavin, proud as his pack moved past him. They feared him. That was what he needed. It was what he wanted.

Kal glanced one more time at what was left of the poor soul who had been unlucky enough to work tonight. He said a silent prayer to his master. Without another word Kal followed Gavin like the obedient puppy that he was.

Chapter 11

The sound of a Citation X on its final approach broke the early morning silence on a private airfield in England. The pilot guided the plane into an empty hanger and the engines quieted. A man rushed up to the plane with a clipboard as he brushed off his shirt.

As the hatch opened, the sound of voices floated out.

"Ok, so tell me again how you decided on this particular aircraft, love."

There was a sigh. "How many times do I have to tell you? It sounded really cool. Say it with me: Cessna Citation X." She hissed the letter X to make it sound cooler. Then she crossed her arms to make an X. "Citation X. See? It's really cool."

Linx shook his head and mumbled, "And you say that I'm weird for the music I like."

As they stepped off the plane, the man with the clipboard and a thick accent greeted them with a smile. "Welcome to England. As always, we will take care of your aircraft until your return. How long will you be staying with us?"

Haydeez paused. "A day or two. We should be finished with our business by then."

"Very good. We will ensure that your aircraft remains secure." He made some notes on his clipboard. "We will have it ready for you tomorrow in case you are done early."

Haydeez nodded and began to walk away. "Is the car out front?" she asked over her shoulder.

The man turned to catch up with her as he desperately tried to impress her. "As always, it's waiting for you in front of the building. Is there anything else that we could do for you during your visit?"

She waved him off and continued on her way.

"Very good," he said as he watched her leave the hanger.

Linx took the driver's seat and they headed away from the airstrip.

"So, where are we headed?" Haydeez said as she flicked through the stations on the radio.

"We're going to get another of those wooden bird things," Linx said with his eyes on the road. "Do you have to do that?" he asked. It sounded like someone continuously clicked a pen. His muscles flinched as he tried to control his irritation.

The stations skipped at a speed so fast anybody who listened would hurt themselves as they tried to decipher what played on each. "Bad day all of the sudden? Don't you think it's important to tell the person who is probably going to be risking her life to get this thing what exactly it is that she'll be up against?" The radio stopped on a station that played oldies and Haydeez sat back to enjoy the music.

"Really? This is what you want to listen to?" Linx asked incredulously. He glanced at her, his face looked like he had just eaten something he did not like.

She held up her hand to stop him. "First, don't change the subject. Second, don't ever say anything bad about one of the greatest voices to ever come out of a person," Haydeez said as she closed her eyes and soaked up every word.

Linx glanced at Haydeez. "Greatest voices? This is the kind of stuff old people listen to, love. You seriously need to upgrade your music collection before you become an old lady yourself." He turned the rental car down a side road as if he had gone this way hundreds of times.

Haydeez eyes shot open and she slowly turned to face Linx, her eyes wide as if he had just insulted her very soul. "There are three voices in music that matter. Ozzy Osbourne because, let's face it, the Ozzman is amazing. Steve Perry, the one and only 'Voice'."

Linx tried to stifle a snicker and failed miserably.

Haydeez ignored him and continued. "And finally, Dean Martin, who can make any word in Italian or English sound like a proposition. And now you can keep your mouth shut until he's finished." She leaned back in her seat.

Several minutes passed with the only sound being the intoxicating voice of Dean Martin. When the song ended, Linx said, "Alright, I'll give you Ozzy. I mean, in his one video when he says 'Too many religions but only one god' and points to himself, that's brilliant. But Steve Perry and Dean Martin? I pegged you for more of a metal head than a love song freak."

"Just because these are the greatest voices to ever be heard does not mean that they are the only ones I listen to, Linx. You've been in my home for how long and you don't even know that. Doesn't say much about our friendship. Besides, you're not a woman. If you heard them through my ears, you'd definitely understand."

The car rolled through a small town and stopped in front of a local restaurant. Linx turned the key and there was silence.

Haydeez looked around. "What are we doing here? Does this place have the bird?"

Linx sighed. "We have to wait for dark. Fancy something to eat? I used to come here all the time. The food's exceptional."

Haydeez paused. "You're from here? Huh, I guess I never really thought about where you used to be before I stole you away from that company. What the heck was it called again?" She opened the door and stood up. "Did you live nearby? We should go by your old house." She closed the door and walked around the Jeep towards the restaurant.

Linx got up and answered, "It was called D.O.G.M.A." The pulse in his head became a constant reminder of where he was. As he closed the door, he said, "Right, let's get something to eat."

•   •   •   •   •

As the sun began to set, Haydeez turned to Linx and said, "Do we have to wait till the witching hour or is early evening dark enough?" She picked at the last few bits of food on her plate.

"Funny. I figured you'd appreciate the cover of darkness. If you want to go now, we'll go now." He stood up and began to walk away.

Haydeez grabbed his arm and halted him immediately. "Listen, little girl. If you're going to have this attitude and get your little girl undies all bunched up, I swear I'll take you out back and beat the ever-loving crap out of you. You know I can take you. Now sit." She forced him back into his seat. "Stop the whining and tell me what the hell is going on right now. You know I hate surprises and this feels like a 'monster behind you in the woods' kind of surprise." She put her foot on the seat next to him to prevent him from sliding back out of the booth.

Linx cleared his throat. "Look, I know who has one of those wooden bird things. I've known them for many years and I know how to get it. I'm not happy about this and I wish I was wrong but I'm not. I remember seeing it when I was young and thinking what a waste it was to have it in the collection. It seemed like just a worthless piece of wood that someone had carved into a stupid bird. If I'd known then that I would need it in the future, I would've taken it and ran."

"So, someone from your childhood has our little birdie. Let's go get it and get out of here. If I have to look at you being all pissy for much longer, I think I'll kill myself." She stood up and headed to the door.

Linx rolled his eyes, grabbed the check, and grudgingly followed.

Chapter 12

The scent of night-blooming jasmine floated on the breeze. A horse whinnied in the distance as Haydeez and Linx climbed an eight foot stone wall.

As she landed on the other side, Haydeez whispered, "Can't you move faster? I'd like to get this over with." She looked up at the top of the wall. "You're sure there's no cameras here, right?" she asked.

Linx began to climb down the wall and lost his footing. He hit the ground with a thump and whispered, "I'm sure, and thanks for your help." He groaned as he tried to stand. "This was so much easier when I was thirteen. I think I broke something just now." He checked his arm and noticed a little trickle of blood. "Fantastic. I'm bleeding now." He ignored the pulse in his head and the blood on his arm and focused on the task.

Haydeez rolled her eyes and said, "Let's go princess."

"Do you care that I breathe?" Linx asked as he dusted himself off. His muscles protested as his blood thumped in his head.

Haydeez chuckled and rolled her eyes again. "Let's just get this over with before we're caught. I find it very hard to believe that someone who purchases and displays valuable items does not have security cameras posted at every possible angle. Something just doesn't seem right here."

Linx took the lead and stepped lightly. "Please pay attention. These are not ordinary collectors. Yes, they purchase valuable items but they also purchase mystically charged, magical items. They know about the stuff we deal with every day. We have to be more careful than usual. Security here is more along the lines of a T-Rex acting as a guard dog."

"A T-Rex huh? So, what, do they experiment on dogs and create mutants that walk the fence lines?" Haydeez snickered. "Watch where you step. Mutant dog poop can be explosive."

"Fine, if you don't believe me, you lead. The house is that way." Linx stopped and pointed. "You get past the creatures, into the display room, recover the bird, and I'll wait here." Linx crossed his arms, stood, and waited for her to move forward. This was the last place he wanted to be. He thought he would never have to set foot on this property again and yet here he was, trudging along in the dark.

She grabbed his arm and dragged him forward. "You make me want to throw something heavy." She let go of his arm and absently waived in front of her. "Ok, so what are these guard creatures and where are they?"

Linx cracked his neck and continued to walk. "They usually roam the property during the day. But at night, they're kept in the stable. It's actually their choice to be in the stable. These things pretty much lock themselves in at night and let themselves out in the morning. If they hear us though, they'll come running and sound the alarm. The only way past them is get them under our control first."

"And I'm guessing you know how to do that," Haydeez said. Her head cocked to the side. "What's up ahead? It's covered in mystical energy. What the hell are we getting into here?"

There was no response as they continued towards to the barn.

When they got closer, Linx motioned Haydeez to stay back while he made his way inside the barn. With a roll of her eyes, she silently agreed. Her body swayed slightly under the pressure of the energy.

"Have you ever noticed that you do that a lot?" Linx whispered.

"Do what?"

"Roll your eyes at me. How about a little trust once in a while?" he asked, a hurt look in his eyes. He turned and disappeared into the barn.

After a few minutes of staring off into space, Haydeez heard the sound of footsteps and saw Linx coming towards her with what looked like silk bridles. "What are those for?"

"The creatures won't bother us now," Linx said. He paused at the surprised look from Haydeez. "Don't worry. I'll put them back before we go." It was his turn to roll his eyes as Haydeez continued to give him a look. "You don't trust me still? Fine, I'll show you that we're safe. Be quiet." He took her by the arm and they walked quietly into the barn.

As they walked through the doors, Haydeez had to do a double take. In three of the stalls stood creatures she'd never encountered, even in her line of work.

Three sets of eyes turned toward the pair. Aside from the odd color, the creatures could be mistaken for normal ordinary horses. Unfortunately for them, the pale blue shimmering fur revealed their true name to Haydeez. The three kelpies stared at her and ignored Linx as he held the bridles.

An odd watery voice spoke. "Would you like a ride? We can run across the open fields with the wind in your hair. I'll take you any place you would like to go," one kelpie said to Haydeez in a low, deep tone. The call of the kelpie was like an invisible hand that tugged on her shirt tail.

She glanced at Linx and asked, "How close is the nearest body of water? I'm not getting dragged under by these things."

"There's a lake on the property. Here," he said as he handed a bridle to Haydeez. "You'll need this to prevent that one from trying to grab you." He eyed the kelpie and said, "You will obey. Haydeez is not your prey." He enunciated every word to ensure his message was understood. His muscles not only protested this time but they began to twitch. Knowing how to stop these creatures was one thing but confronting them and giving them an order was another. It was at that moment that he realized he had no idea how they were going to put the bridles back and get off the property without getting caught. He pushed aside the thought in the hope that he would think of something before that moment came.

The kelpie clicked its backward facing hoof and shook its mane. Its fur glittered like a breeze dancing across water in the moonlight. The creature gave Linx a dirty look and walked back into one of the stalls.

"We best get out of here before our luck runs out," Linx whispered. "These bridles control the kelpies. They'll prevent them from trying to drag us into that lake. I'll put them back before we go." He grabbed Haydeez by the arm again and pulled her quietly out into the night.

Without another word, she tucked the soft bridle into her jacket. It was not an ordinary bridle. It was made of spun spider silk, a material stronger than Kevlar, and held a powerful magic within its woven strands. She clutched it through her jacket to make sure it was still hidden. They continued to walk towards the house with Linx in the lead, the other bridles tucked safely into his jacket pockets.

After several moments of silence, Linx turned to Haydeez and said, "We have to be quiet up here. The kelpies aren't the only things guarding this place. Wait here," Linx whispered.

"Again," Haydeez mumbled and rolled her eyes.

"Stop that," Linx whispered. He knew what she had done without so much as a glance in her direction. Linx walked to the back door and knocked quietly. The door opened and a tiny creature waited on the inside. It was dressed in brown clothing and stood only three feet tall.

"A brownie? You have got to be kidding me." Haydeez stared at the doorway in anticipation of a problem. "Those things are so finicky. Why would someone want one in their house?"

"I think I'll leave these oats by the door and then go in to take a look at the family collection," Linx looked inside but above the brownie's head. It looked as if he was talking to himself.

Before it could respond, Linx turned and added, "My friend will be coming in for a little visit as well." He motioned for Haydeez to come forward.

She stood next to Linx. He quickly whispered, "Don't talk to it. Just walk inside and be quiet."

"I really don't like being told what to do. You do know I'm going to hurt you when we get home." Haydeez gave him a dirty look and walked past him into the kitchen of the house.

Linx motioned Haydeez to follow him. They walked through the house without a sound. Linx heard a voice and stopped. "Damn," he mumbled under his breath. "In here. We'll grab the bird and wait." He pulled Haydeez into a room. His pulse raced and his stomach flip-flopped.

"You never did tell me how you knew about this place. I mean, I know it's from your childhood in some way but," she said.

"Not now. Later," he whispered. He covered her mouth with his hand. Her eyes were wide with shock.

When the voice faded, Linx turned and looked around the room. He pulled a small pen light from a pocket and clicked it on. A thin sliver of light moved around the room. "It should be over here in this case." He walked to the far wall and looked into a glass box. In the middle of the case sat a hand carved bird. The tiny eagle with its wings spread seemed to be the focal point of the case.

Linx's eyes slid over the other pieces and fell on another hand carved item. His heart skipped a beat. "There're two. They have two birds. Haydeez, they have the owl. We've got three carvings now. We only need the other two," he whispered excitedly. He turned to see the shadow of Haydeez pinned to a wall by the wrong end of a shotgun.

Chapter 13

"You have nothing, my dear boy. Those items belong to me and not..." the voice trailed off as the light to the room clicked on. "Oh, Maximillian Xavier Van Martin, if you were coming for a visit, you should've called." At the other end of the shotgun stood an older man. "Should I let your little friend go? It's against my better judgment considering you were intending to rob your own parents but we are family after all," the man said as he clicked the safety into place.

"Maximillian Xavier?" Haydeez snickered. "Oh we are so talking about this later." She tried to stifle a laugh and failed.

"Shut it. Now you know why I call myself Linx, why I know my way around the place, and how I could find the second piece. By the way, did you hear me say I found the third one too or were you too busy laughing at my birth name?" he asked. He turned to his father and asked, "Do you really expect me to call ahead when you tried to have me killed the last time I was here? I hardly had time to collect my things and get off the property before your psycho kelpies tried to take me to the lake." He swallowed hard as he remembered the day he left home.

His father laughed. "Oh that was just a misunderstanding, son. We weren't really trying to kill you. That's just silly. Have a seat." He motioned to a couch in the middle of the room. "Would you like something to drink?"

Linx glared at his father. "Right. I'd love something to drink, and I would love for you to make it yourself with a little something extra added. If I wanted to kill myself, I wouldn't have grabbed this," he pulled part of a bridle from his jacket, "before I came up to the house. I know how you are, father." He sat on the couch. "So, now what? You shoot us and feed us to your creatures?"

His father rolled his eyes. "I was upset when you left but I certainly didn't try to kill you. I never gave them an order to hunt you down. They did that on their own." He put the gun against his shoulder. "Son, you never even told us where you were going or why you were leaving or anything. We were worried and concerned. Had you just sat down with us and talked, perhaps we wouldn't be having this conversation at this very moment. Now, that drink..." his voice trailed off. "Wait, you said something about a bird."

"It's nothing of interest to you. I just need to take a couple of birds with me when we go." Linx looked defiantly at his father. "I could call in my kelpie friends to get them or you could just let me take them. It's entirely up to you." He leaned forward with his elbows on his knees and his hands clasped. "What do you say?"

"Max, is this really necessary? There's really no need to act like we're your enemy." He turned to Haydeez and said, "He was like this as a child as well. He always wanted to stay inside and play with his little machines. I would try to get him to go hunting with me and he would tell me he would send the boogie man after me if I made him go." He chuckled. "He really has quite a little fire inside. He gets that from his mother."

Haydeez chuckled again as she turned to Linx. "Ah, family reunions are such fun." A mocking smile spread across her lips as she watched Linx twitch and squirm.

"By the way dear, my son is terribly rude. I'm Max Senior." He reached out his hand. "And you're his girlfriend?" he asked, an edge of hope in his voice.

Haydeez laughed as she reached out and shook his hand. "Call me Haydeez and we work together, that's all. So he's a junior then? Makes the names even longer doesn't it?" she asked with a smile.

"No, just Linx remember?" Linx answered before his father could speak. "Could we please just get the birds and go already? It's not like we got all the time in the world or anything, Haydeez. We're kind of on a schedule." He stood up and moved to the case with the wooden bird carvings. "Are you going to unlock these for me or what?"

Max Sr. looked at Haydeez and sighed. "He really hasn't changed one bit. You really must come back when your mother's here. She left to look for a relic of some kind. I think it was some Egyptian crown thing. Anyway, if you want them, take them. I'm missing part of the set anyway. I hate having incomplete sets and I have no idea where the other pieces are," he said. He looked at Haydeez and added, "My wife never really liked them anyway. She said they had a strange feel to them, as if they were hiding a curse or holding a soul prisoner. She'll be happy to be rid of them when she returns."

"The key, father," Linx said, impatience in his voice. "We have to leave."

Max Sr. walked over to the case and pulled a ring of keys from his robe pocket. He flipped through them and found the correct key.

After his father unlocked the case, Linx lifted the lid and removed the two wooden birds, an eagle in flight and a resting owl, and gently wrapped them in separate cloths to protect them from scratches. He did not really believe that they could be damaged but now would be a bad time to be wrong. He walked to Haydeez and handed them to her.

As they turned to walk out the door, Linx's father said, "The bridles, Max. I'd like them back." He held out his hand and waited.

Linx smiled. "Do you really believe that I'd just hand them over when we still have to make it off the property? I'll return them to their place before we leave. You can trust me. I'm not the one who tried to kill someone, remember?" He turned and began to walk out the door.

"Right, you're just the one stealing from your family," Max Sr mumbled to himself as he watched his son leave the room. "Good to see you again, son," he called after them.

They left the house without incident. When they reached the barn, Linx took the third bridle from Haydeez and said, "Start walking towards the wall. I'll put these back and catch up with you."

Haydeez nodded and walked towards the back of the property.

Linx went into the barn. He walked to a reinforced room with a keypad and entered a code. The door beeped and he reached for the handle.

A voice broke the silence. "Hello again, boy. Welcome back." The kelpie from earlier had its eyes fixed on Linx.

"Don't talk to me, creature. I know your tricks. I'm not falling for them tonight," Linx said and turned back to the door.

"As soon as your fingers leave the silk, I will be on you in an instant. Your skin will be mine. All they'll find is your puny heart floating on the surface of the lake. You escaped once. Not this time, boy. I'll eat your flesh this night." It clicked its hooves and whinnied. The shimmering fur bristled like the wind passed over it.

Linx paused for a moment. He thought about his options. He was near the door to the barn and could try to run for it after he put down the bridles. But the question was: could he make it to the wall?

He brushed off his anxiety and took a deep breath before he entered the code again and opened the door. His eyes darted to the kelpie who had not moved its gaze from him. With a quick glance into the room, he tossed the bridles and ran.

Wood cracked and splintered as the kelpie broke free from the stall. The sound hit his ears like a sonic boom. He focused his eyes forward and flew through the door of the barn. He picked up speed as he ran. His heart raced and his body told him to move faster. Without a thought he screamed, "Run, Haydeez! Run for the wall!"

Haydeez turned and saw Linx pound the ground behind her. A second later she saw the kelpie come up behind him as well. The blood drained from her face and she gasped. Her body spun and she began to run. "What the hell did you do?" she yelled over her shoulder.

"Just bloody run!" Linx yelled back.

They wove in and out of the trees and over roots with the kelpie in tow. Linx caught up with Haydeez and slowly began to pass her. "Run faster! You don't want to end up in the lake!" he yelled as he passed her.

"You better not let me die! I will haunt you!" she yelled back as she pushed herself faster. Goosebumps rippled across her skin. The kelpie's magic was close. She became suddenly aware that she was further behind Linx with each stride. Fear prickled all over her body. She had almost collapsed in the barn after being close to all three of the creatures. With that single thought, she forced her legs to pump harder.

That same watery voice floated to her ears. "Your skin will taste extra sweet. Fear adds flavor. I'll savor you tonight." The hooves pounded the dirt right behind them. Linx could feel the power too now.

Haydeez yelled at Linx. "I am so not dying here." She breathed in deep and let it out with a grunt. She picked up speed. "That damn wall seemed a lot closer when we got here," she groaned.

Linx laughed and slowed. "Don't do that!" He jumped over a large root. "Oi! Just keep running!"

The wall loomed in the darkness in front of them. Linx leapt up onto the wall and scrambled up. He sat on the top and watched as Haydeez took a flying leap. She scratched her way up until something caught her foot. She whipped her head around to see the kelpie's muzzle stuck to her ankle.

"You have got to be kidding me!" she yelled. "Pull me up!"

Linx turned pale and grabbed her hand. He ignored the ache in his legs and balanced himself but he knew. "Once you're stuck, I can't do anything," he whispered. He pulled on her in a futile attempt to rescue her.

"The hell you can't! Pull damnit! This thing is *not* going to eat me!" She tried to pull herself up. Her muscles burned as she pulled harder. She could feel her leg muscles strain as they stretched between the kelpie and Linx. Her eyes met Linx and she whispered, "Help me. I don't want to die."

Linx just stared with her hand clasped in his. "I can't." Everything in his brain told him that there was nothing he could do but he couldn't bring himself to let her go.

"Jesus Christ, Linx!" Haydeez yelled. As soon as she spoke, her foot was released and the two of them flew over the top of the wall. They landed with a thud and a crunch on the other side of the wall. "What the hell happened?"

Linx groaned from under Haydeez. "I think I broke something." He squirmed and screamed. "That's my arm! Bloody hell! I think I broke my arm!"

Haydeez rolled off Linx and slowly pushed herself up. "Thanks for being my cushion," she joked. "Can you stand or do I have to carry you?" She smiled.

"Bugger off," he mumbled as he pulled himself up with his one good arm.

She put her arm around his waist and helped him steady himself.

Chapter 14

"I don't care if they're tired. The sooner we reach our destination, the sooner we can rest. Once we're released from Cernunnous's grasp, we can run free and do as we please," Gavin growled as he paced. "Must I make an example of these useless pups?" he asked. His anger pulsed around him like a heater set to high.

In a small forest in central England, the pack rested. They had moved for almost twenty-four hours straight. They stopped only to hunt. They panted and laid on the ground covered in sweat. Most remained in dog form to expend as little energy as possible. The few who were strong enough to turn back to human curled up alongside the rest of the pack with their eyes closed in the hopes that their Alpha would allow them to rest.

Kal looked at Gavin. "My Alpha, I don't believe that lessening our numbers would be wise at this time. Perhaps I should speak to them and convey the importance of our quest. After all, I wouldn't have you bother yourself with such a menial task." Kal hoped that Gavin would agree and spare his friends.

Gavin let out a low rumble and fixed his eyes on Kal. "Advise them of the need to finish this as soon as possible. If they can't understand, I'll be forced to make them understand." His heat washed over Kal.

With a quick nod, Kal said, "Yes, my Alpha," and turned. He made his way to a small group of people and told them what the Alpha had said. With a collective shudder, tears welled up and they agreed.

Kal returned to convey the response.

A toothy grin spread across his lips as Gavin said, "I knew my pack wasn't stupid. They appreciate the hunt as their Alpha does. Come. It's time we moved on. Our destiny awaits."

Kal bowed slightly and turned to alert the others.

Gavin felt the sigh that rippled across the pack as each member stood. They were obviously not ready to continue their trip. Those who had requested rest remained at the back of the group, to avoid being near the Alpha. In spite of their placement, he already knew who they were and watched their every move.

Gavin reached into his shirt and removed a necklace. He had left everything personal with his car in Canada except this. He rubbed the charm and whispered, "We're coming for you, *Master.*" He spat the last word in disgust. "No longer will I be your servant. I'll be free." He ran his finger over the wooden stag in his hand and smiled. "I'll find you soon and then I'll destroy you for everything you've done."

Chapter 15

"I'm fine. Honestly, it doesn't even hurt anymore."

"Do you really think I'm that stupid? I can handle this on my own. You have to stay here. If you move, I'll beat you."

"Promise?" An evil grin spread across his lips as he watched Haydeez flatten the sheets and fluff his pillows. He sat on his bed in the hotel with a cast on his arm. "I can't believe you let me get hurt. And I was trying to save you too. This is the thanks I get for helping you." He faked a pout.

Haydeez gave Linx a dirty look. "It's not my fault that you can't hold on, Humpty Dumpty. Just be happy in the knowledge that you provided a soft landing for me." She smiled and left the room.

"That's really not how I pictured the first time you were on top of me, love," he called after her.

A muffled voice called back. "Stay in bed or else."

Linx laughed to himself and settled into the warm mound of pillows behind his back.

Haydeez walked down the hall to the elevator. She tried to make sense of everything that had happened. She had three of the pieces to release Cernunnous but had no idea where to find the other two or his prison for that matter.

"Pandora is the one releasing all these things. The question is why. What's she trying to do? What does she want?" Haydeez whispered to herself as she pressed the button for the first floor. "I understand the whole 'downfall of man' thing but how does she intend to do it? Ugh, I need food to help me think."

Her phone buzzed in her pocket. Surprised to have a signal in the elevator, she reached in to check the number. Her shoulders dropped. She pressed the button to answer it and said, "Peter, how nice of you to call."

A man's voice on the other side answered, "You haven't delivered the creature yet. When were you planning on contacting us?" His voice carried an Italian lilt.

She sighed. "There's been a minor change in plans. My price went up."

There was a laugh on the other end. "You're in no position to negotiate after we've agreed upon a contract. We'll pay you what we agreed on and nothing more."

Haydeez stepped out of the elevator and scanned the lobby. She saw a restaurant entrance in the distance. "No, you'll pay me five times what we agreed on and nothing less. You see, it's come to my attention that more of these little creatures are running around wreaking havoc in the same area. It's no longer a single nuisance. It's five. So, if you want all this nonsense to stop, you and your little group will pay me what I want."

There was silence on the line.

"That's ok. You boys talk it over and you let me know what you decide. How's that sound?" Haydeez asked. She walked over to the restaurant and scanned the menu.

"Wait," Peter said reluctantly. A hint of irritation entered his voice as he continued. "It appears that the situation has changed and we may need to re-negotiate the terms of our deal. My colleagues and I agree that this issue needs to be handled. We feel that it would be in our best interest to offer you an increase in your pay if you would agree to capture the extra creatures. We're prepared to offer you five times what we had originally agreed upon. Is this acceptable for you?" he asked. He made it sound as if he and these other unseen men had come to the same conclusion on their own and made the offer to Haydeez.

"Well Peter, you certainly drive a hard bargain but I believe we've come to an agreement. I'll call you once I've rounded them up. Will I be seeing your happy smiling face this time or just another of your lackeys again?" she asked.

"No," he answered.

She heard the phone click. She thought about all the cleanup she did for Peter and his little group. She was curious about who they were and where the money came from until it ended up in her bank account. Once she saw all the little zeroes, the curiosity seemed to subside. After all, this was a job like any other.

•　　•　　•　　•　　•

Haydeez read over all her notes for the fifth time. She tried to find a connection between Pandora and the creatures that had been released.

Nothing stood out to her. The creatures had nothing to do with each other. They were not even from the same mythology as Pandora. Nothing made sense.

She groaned. "What the hell is going on?" She dropped her head on the table with a thud.

"Maybe I can help?" a voice quietly broke the silence.

"Get back to bed," Haydeez said without lifting her head.

Linx moved the covers aside and swung his feet to the floor. "You could make me or you could let me help like I'm supposed to be doing. Your choice, love," he said.

Haydeez groaned again. "Fine. Sit. Help." She lifted her head and handed him her notes.

"Is this everything?" he asked. She nodded. "Alright, let's see what we've got."

He read through everything twice. When he put down the papers, he said, "On the surface, I can't find a connection either. We need to look past everything we know to the stuff that we're just guessing."

"You want to just make up a reason for what's happening? How does that even make sense?" she asked.

Linx stood up. "Ok, stay with me for a minute. We obviously don't know what she's planning, right? Unless we actually find her and talk to her we'll never know what she's actually doing. All we can do at this point is guess what her next move is. We know she released Robley and his friends and they know about the missing babies. Is that a coincidence? Maybe but I doubt it.

"What if she released him and the others like him so they could take babies? So, part of her plan has to do with kidnapping babies. See where I'm going with this?" he asked.

Haydeez nodded. "Ok, so she wants babies. Now what? We've been hunting these wooden pieces to release this trapped god, Cernunnous, so he can take back control of his pack from who or whatever has them now. Who can take control of the pack?" she mused.

"Another god maybe," Linx said.

"Not likely," Haydeez said. "Remember, Lian said all those other gods were imprisoned long ago. It's not likely to be one of them." She thought for a moment and said, "There really shouldn't be anything else that can take control like that. If he has a connection to his pack, nothing short of killing the god should break that connection." She stopped and turned to Linx, a light clicked on inside her head. Her eyes focused on Linx. "But in his absence, the pack would work like any military operation. In the absence of a commanding officer, the second in command would take charge. The pack has to have an alpha." She smiled triumphantly. "They'd work like a regular wolf pack mixed with a military hierarchy."

Linx began to pace. "So who's the alpha?"

"I have no idea," Haydeez said. "But at least now we know who's controlling the pack." She excitedly added some notes to her papers. "But why is the alpha acting now? I mean, if the pack's been hiding out in Canada for all these years, why, all of a sudden, are they travelling across the ocean back to a home they ran away from? Why would they want to go back to a god they wanted to get away from?" Haydeez asked.

Linx grabbed the phone and dialed. "I think I might know why." He waited while the phone connected on the other end. "Keeglian, I have a question for you, mate." He paused. He put up a finger to Haydeez to wait. He did not want to have to repeat everything. "Ok, so you said before that this god, Cernunnous, was locked up by the Christians, right? Well, is it possible that his Alpha got sucked into Pandora's Box at some point?" he asked as he looked directly at Haydeez. "Right, that's what we thought. If the Alpha got sucked in, Pandora could have easily released him. So we could be going after the Alpha of Cernunnous's pack, the most powerful creature under the god's control." Linx smiled proudly and then quickly frowned. "Oh bollocks. I really wish I hadn't figured that out."

Haydeez laughed. "We would've eventually figured it out. The problem we have now is how to stop an indestructible wolf."

Linx listened. "What do you mean? The pack's from the British Isles, not Canada." He stopped for a minute. "Hold on." He put the phone on speaker and set it on the counter. "You want to start over again, Keeglian."

The familiar voice crackled through the speaker. "Think about who settled Canada. You think of Canada as its own separate country but you forget that the Crown still holds control of certain parts. It's a colony of the British Isles. Now think of the most powerful canine in our mythology. A god would want to have a creature almost as strong and powerful as he to stand by his side. He would want someone who could easily slip from the human life to canine life." Keeglian waited for a response. "Is anyone even listening anymore?" he asked.

"Of course. We're just waiting for you to tell us," Haydeez said with a snicker. "You know how I hate to figure things out on my own." She quietly laughed.

"Quite. I've heard stories of what the Green Man picked for his alpha but the creature that seemed most prominent in the stories was the Loup Garou. It can change without the full moon and stands almost eight feet tall." He paused. "The Loup Garou can change into a half man, half wolf creature. Most likely, if this is who's controlling the pack, you'll need help. You can't take him on by yourself," Keeglian said.

Haydeez looked at Linx and said, "Well, it looks like I'm going to have to because my backup's out of commission at the moment. I've dealt with some pretty bad creatures over the years. I think I can handle it."

"You think you can but trust me when I say that you won't," Keeglian said. "You can't win, ducky. You're not indestructible. You *can* be hurt and you *can* die." He was silent for a moment.

"Has everyone forgotten that we specialize in the impossible? We fight mythological creatures and things from your nightmares. Why can't we take on one bloody werewolf?" Linx asked.

Keeglian sighed heavily. "First of all, it's not a werewolf. It's called a Loup Garou. Werewolves change with the lunar cycle. The Loup Garou changes at will and can take on any form between and including full human and full wolf. Second, it's not a matter of your skill, boy. The creature can't die unless his master takes away his immortality. The Green Man is the only one who can stop the Alpha. You must understand this fact before you take another step. If you ignore this, you'll most certainly die," Keeglian said, a hint of anger in his voice this time. "I don't like most people, Haydeez. You know that and I have no intention of sending you to your death. You've ignored my warnings in the past and you got lucky. Luck is not on your side this time."

"So what do you expect me to do, 'Lian? If I just ignore all this, Pandora wins. She'll destroy man. What do you suggest I do?" Haydeez asked, her anger a match for Keeglian. She hated when people tried to protect her like she was a delicate child.

"I *expect you* to handle this. You must wake up the god to take care of his dogs. You must find Cernunnous, release him from his prison, and get him to take back control of his pack." Keeglian said. "That's your only chance. Pandora must not win." He tried not to raise his voice but the frustration got the better of him. Sometimes, it was like he spoke to a chair. He could talk all he wanted to, but that chair was not going to listen to anything he had to say.

Haydeez just stared at the phone for a moment. Then she said, "Well, then I guess that's what I have to do. Linx, hit the computer and see if you can find a possible location for Cernunnous. Also, see if you can find the last two pieces. I need those to get him out of whatever he's in." She picked up the phone. "Thanks, 'Lian. I'll keep you updated. If the world ends, you know I failed."

"Funny. I find you to be very humorous. Don't fail, and call me when you're done." Keeglian hung up without waiting for a response.

Haydeez looked at Linx. "What are you waiting for?"

Linx just looked at her. "Aren't you worried? He said you can't win." He started to get nervous.

Haydeez scoffed. "He says that a lot. I'll be fine. You worry enough for the both of us."

"Haydeez, you've got to be more careful. He's right. You're not indestructible. You take a lot of unnecessary risks. Think about what just happened with a bloody kelpie. I know you're scared to die."

"Are you my mother now? Look, I do what has to be done. If my life's at risk, then that's what needs to happen. There are things in this world that don't belong and nobody else is going to do anything about it. So, I guess that leaves me. I'm it, Linx. Just do your job and let me do mine." She walked out of the room and let the door slam behind her. Inside she knew he was right but she could not let it get to her. She had to do this. As soon as she let those thoughts in, that was the end. She would slip up, get hurt, and get herself killed, or worse. She might get Linx killed and she was not about to let that happen.

Linx sighed. "Fine. I'll just shut up and do my bloody job then." He picked up one of the wooden pieces. The eagle's wings reached out across his palm. The wood shimmered and pulsed with power. It felt warm like a cookie fresh from the oven.

He picked up the owl and looked at the eyes. Lifeless orbs looked back at him. He held the bird in his palm and cocked his head to the side. His brow furrowed and he said, "What the hell..." He rolled it around in his hand for a moment. "Now that's not right," he said to himself. He picked up the first piece they found and compared the two.

"Haydeez!" he yelled. "Get back here now! Something's wrong!" He stood up with the owl and ran to the door. "Haydeez! It's not real! The owl's a fake."

Chapter 16

Haydeez turned around slowly. "What do you mean it's a fake? Let me see that." She grabbed the owl out of Linx's hands to inspect it.

The details were just as specific and ornate. Each little feather held texture. She could even make out the large vein down the middle of the bigger feathers. The eyes, however, looked back at her without any life or expression as she brought it up close to her face. The wood was made out of the same type of tree but not the same tree.

"How did this happen? How did they not notice that this was a complete fake?" Haydeez asked. She squeezed the owl in her fist.

Linx shook his head. "Maybe they knew. I mean, my father never 'collected' anything that was... ordinary. His collection consists of the kind of stuff you'd read about in fantasy novels or the mythology section of the library. Everything in there has its own story or its own legend about what it may or may not do." He shook his head again. "No, he had to know. There has to be something about this piece that made him want it."

She turned to punch the wall and stopped herself. "Damn! I hate losing ground. Now we still need three pieces to release him and we don't even know where he is. Damn!" She leaned against the wall. "Any ideas yet why he would've wanted this one?" she said as she tossed the fake owl back to Linx.

He caught it with one hand and said, "Nothing yet but I'm sure I'll figure it out." He looked at the eyes again. "Lousy dead eyes." He put his finger on one and pushed like he was poking it.

The face rotated slightly as he put pressure on it. He gasped and his eyes grew wide.

"Oi! It moved." He held it out to show Haydeez. "Watch this." He pushed on the eye again, this time he tried to rotate it intentionally. The face turned again and then popped off. Linx removed the piece and showed Haydeez. "It's a hidden compartment."

"Thank you, Captain Obvious," Haydeez said.

"Did you find it? No, no you didn't. So back off," Linx said with a fake sneer. "And if you're done making fun of me..." He trailed off as he turned back to the owl. "There's something inside." He pulled out a small piece of paper no larger than his finger. He unfolded it and read it. "Oh come on. It's a bloody riddle."

"Please tell me you're joking," she said.

Linx shook his head.

"Great, a treasure hunt. And I thought this was going to be easy," Haydeez said with a laugh as she reached out her hand. "Ok, let's see it then."

Linx handed her the thin piece of delicate paper. He looked over her shoulder as she read the riddle.

"The eyes of the night watch o'er her King in the Isle of Avalon." She read as she walked back to the room.

"Please tell me you misread that. 'The Isle of Avalon'? As in King Arthur?" Linx exclaimed. "That's England." He paused. "What are the eyes of the night though?" His mind was racing.

Haydeez looked at him. "I'm guessing it's an owl, the owl we're looking for, the little wooden birdy," she said sarcastically.

"Oh, right. Owls see better at night. Makes sense I suppose," he said defeated. "Ready for a treasure hunt?"

Haydeez walked over to the laptop and began typing. "I'm as ready as I'll ever be. As soon as I figure out what the Isle of Avalon is, I'll be out the door."

Linx smiled, a renewed energy flowed from him. "Great. I'll get dressed. You'll probably want to change and freshen up."

"Freeze," Haydeez said without looking up. "This is a 'me' trip, not a 'we' trip. You're still broken. I can't have you getting yourself even more banged up. You stay." She continued to type, her eyes never left the screen.

"Right. And then halfway there you'll miss me and wish that I was there with you. No worries, love. I'll be right there with you already. Besides it's been a few days. I'm feeling quite well now," Linx said. "You know you can't get along without me. Who'll make your tea?"

"I hate tea."

"Blasphemy."

"You're not going."

"Stop me."

"Don't make me hurt you."

"Promise?"

"Get dressed," she said as she rolled her eyes.

"You can't resist me," he said victoriously as he pulled out clean clothes.

"I can," she said as she stuck out her tongue in childish defeat.

Haydeez began to pull up any information she could get that might lead her to what she needed.

The first bit of material was a restaurant called "The Wise Salmon". It was in a mountain town in Canada. The area was in a place that was predominantly French. She bookmarked the site but thought it to be a dead end.

Several other places came up that showed locations for salmon fishing and salmon migration studies, all of which proved to be useless.

Finally, she came across a small pub called "Fintan's Place". She pulled up some pictures on a local website. It was a small pub decorated in traditional Irish items, unlike those places that try to be Irish but only pull off the cliché. It was located in a modest town in Northern Ireland. It looked like the type of place that only the locals would frequent.

"Linx can check this out. It'll give him something to do while I look for the owl," she said to herself.

"What can I check?" he asked from the door to the bathroom.

"This little pub…"

"I'm there," he said before she could finish.

She laughed. "Don't you want to know why I'm sending you there?"

He walked over to her chair and leaned down. "No need. I knew you'd miss me, love. Now you don't have to come back to get me." He smiled a toothy grin and wiggled his eyebrows. "What's the name of this joint?"

"Fintan's Place," she said and leaned back. "Local pub in Northern Ireland. We're somewhere in the middle. You hit the pub. I'll take the tower. Hopefully we'll both get lucky."

He looked at the screen and said with a smirk, "All you have to do is ask."

She elbowed him and added, "Find the salmon. When I find the owl, all we'll need is the stag. Hopefully it won't be hard to find Cernunnous. Keeglian's working on it right now. He said he'll let me know if anything comes up." She paused. "Wow, nothing?"

"You have to let some of them go," he said with a smirk. "So, how long till we leave?"

•   •   •   •   •

"Somewhere between, huh?" Linx sped up the highway. He had been on the road for about two hours. Most of that time had been spent complaining to himself. "So I have to drive nine hours to get to some pub while she drives less than an hour. How does that seem fair?"

They had walked outside to separate vehicles when Haydeez looked at Linx and said, "It's nine hours that way," and pointed north.

"You're so lucky I don't hit girls," he said as he gripped the steering wheel harder. His knuckles turned white and his blood was racing. "Whether I find the fish or not, I'm getting pissed and I'm not driving back till tomorrow." He sped around a compact. "We'll see if it takes me nine hours." The speedometer read 140km/h.

Chapter 17

By the time Linx arrived, it was around lunch and his body made sure he knew it. He had not stopped the entire time except once to fill up the tank. His stomach growled and his head throbbed. He pulled out his phone and sent a quick message to let Haydeez know that he was there. He did not bother to wait for a response before going inside because he was still upset about the drive up here.

In the darkness, four sets of eyes watched the door open and the stranger walk inside. The men became silent and continued to stare with disapproval and contempt.

"What do ya want?" the man behind the bar asked.

"Lunch would be preferable but I'll take a pint for now," Linx said, completely unaffected by the men, or at least he hid it well because nobody seemed to notice how nervous he was. He sat on a stool at the bar and waited.

"Ya better be able to pay, lad," the barman said. He hesitantly pulled out a glass and began to fill it.

Linx pulled cash out of his pocket. "That enough?" He slapped it down on the counter. "What do you have to eat?"

•   •   •   •   •

"No woman is worth that kind of trouble, lad. If she's wearing the pants, you'd best find yourself another one," the man sitting next to Linx said. He took a drink and looked longingly into the glass, remembering decisions of the past. "Sometimes I wish I'd taken me own advice." He laughed.

His drunken laughter was met with the laughter of the other men in the pub. One man added, "Ay! Don't we all!"

Linx looked around and thought there was no better time to bring up the salmon. So he asked, in a roundabout way. "Got a lot of fish stuff in here.

Do you have any kind of fish for sale? She's got a thing for fish and it might win me some points if I bring something for her collection." He looked around at the decorations like he was trying to find something to buy in his supposedly inebriated state. His eyes were as sharp as ever though and they spotted something very out of place.

On the far wall, there was a plaque. It had an incredibly intricate image carved into it of a stream in the trees and a bear watching the water. Right in the dead center sat a raised piece of wood carved into the shape of a salmon. It was leaping from the stream as if it were reaching for the sun. It shimmered a little, even in the dim lighting. That was what he came for, he could feel it.

With a little wobble on the stool, he asked, "What about that? "How much do you want for that plaque," he said as he pointed to it, hanging silently on the wall. He gripped the bar, pretending to be too drunk to hold himself upright.

The barman followed where he pointed and said, "I don't know, lad. Great granddad carved it himself. It's been in the family. Don't think I could let it go."

Linx pulled out more money and put it on the counter. "Are you sure I couldn't change your mind?" His words slurred slightly. He blinked a few times, pretending to clear his vision. In spite of the show he was putting on, he was still very much alert and aware of everything going on in the room.

The man suspiciously looked at the money and then at Linx again. He knew something was up the moment this stranger walked in the door and now, this confirmed his apprehensions. "No, lad. I think I'll pass." He eyed Linx cautiously.

Linx shrugged, nearly fell to the floor, and said, "Right then. I thought I'd try," he said with a crooked smile. "I've got to find the bog." He stood up and grabbed the edge of the bar with his good hand to steady himself. With a chuckle and an apology he walked a crooked line to the back wall where the restroom was. He bumped into the wall a few times, mumbling, "Excuse me, mate."

The men ignored him and went about their business. By the time they noticed the missing plaque, Linx had managed to maneuver himself out the bathroom window, despite his arm still being in a sling, and was running for the rental car.

•   •   •   •   •

Gunshots rang out in the early evening air. Four angry Irishmen shouted at Linx's taillights as he sped off.

"Please don't shoot my car. I forgot to get the insurance," he shouted back at them. His fingers raced over the keys on the cell phone while he held the steering wheel with his knees. There were a few rings, then voicemail picked up and Linx groaned. After the beep he said, "I got it. This bloody thing better work. I almost got my head blown off. Pick up your phone and call me back. I'll be on the road the rest of the day." He hung up and tossed the phone on the seat next to the plaque. His arm was throbbing from climbing out the window and he wished he could just take a handful of painkillers and a very long nap.

He glanced at the fish. "You better be worth all the trouble." He eyed the road, not wanting to see if anyone was following. His heart raced and a dull ache crept up in the back of his head but he did not dare stop.

Chapter 18

Haydeez stepped out of her rental and looked around. Beautiful green fields rolled out around her. Stone walkways circled around the grounds. Off in the distance, atop a hill, stood a stone tower. She reached in the back seat and pulled out a backpack. "Now's as good a time as any," she said to herself. "Let's get this over with." She started calmly walking towards the hill.

The sign at the entrance said CLOSED DUE TO RENOVATIONS. This was good for her because nobody would be milling around. She hoped she could get in and get the figure without incident. She laughed to herself. "Right. No problems. I have problems ordering pizza."

She walked with purpose in her steps. This would be the third piece. Linx would find the fourth and all they would need is the stag. They started to get back on track finally. After Linx got hurt when he fell off the wall for those other two pieces and then they found out the owl was a fake, Haydeez thought she had lost for sure. But now, it felt like everything started to make sense. It should all come together. Her brain told her not to be so naïve but she kept thinking it would be a nice change to get through this without thinking she might die.

Her soft-soled moccasins made no sound on the stone. The fresh scent of the earth filled her nostrils, relaxing her muscles, calming her senses. She took the last few steps to the tower and stopped. She breathed in heavily. All of the sudden, something in the air felt wrong. She remembered what it felt like in the little village in Canada and shuddered. Something was here and it was not ordinary. She could not place the feeling but whatever it was caused her to doubt her mission for a second. Uncertainty or not, there was no way she could stop now.

Haydeez walked into the tower and looked around. She closed her eyes and touched the walls, feeling for the power emanating from the piece. Her breathing slowed as she exhaled slowly. Her mind cleared like the fog in the early morning as it slowly burns off with the rays from the rising sun. She concentrated on the sound of her own heartbeat.

Her fingertips ran over the smooth grey stone. Cold tendrils touched her mind as she searched for a warm, earthy energy beneath the walls. There was no power inside.

She followed the wall all the way around back to where she came in and opened her eyes. "Figures. It's up in the tower itself," she mumbled. "Good thing I came prepared." She dropped her backpack and crouched on the ground.

Within minutes, she had strapped herself into a harness. She grabbed the grappling hook and swung it around before she tossed it up the open air tower. It clanked against the stone and hooked on the edge of the opening. "Ha! First try," she laughed proudly as she looked around. "And I'm talking to myself."

After tugging on the rope to make sure it was secure, Haydeez hopped up and began to pull herself up. Hand over hand, she climbed up the rope, grunting the whole time until she was in the actual tower. Her arm muscles bunched with each pull while her legs stretched. Her mind remained empty of all thought except climbing and finding the owl. She reached out and touched a stone, feeling for the piece.

A strong energy pulsed above her and she smiled to herself. The warmth called to her from above. It was a calm, inviting feeling and she pulled herself up a little further. She looked up and saw the owl imbedded in the stone. Her heart started racing, her prize in sight. She climbed a few more feet and clipped the rope in place so she would not slide down. In front of her face was the piece looking back at her with eyes that seemed alive with knowledge and authority. She felt a little uneasy for a moment, unable to pull her gaze away.

She shook her head to clear it and reached around her back to pull a knife from a hidden sheath. With the knife grasped firmly in one hand, she used the point to pry the owl piece from the stone, holding her other out to grab it before it fell.

A triumphant smile spread across her lips as the piece popped out into her hand. She reached back, replaced the knife, slid the piece into a pocket, and zipped the pocket. As she moved to release the rope, she heard a noise that made her muscles freeze and her heart stop.

Stone scraped against stone and echoed up the tower. An unnatural grainy growl rumbled the walls. There was a tug on the rope from below.

Haydeez took a deep breath and tried to prepare herself. She expected to see someone down on the ground waiting for her to come down so they could take the piece. When she looked down to see what had a hold on the line, her jaw dropped and her heart jumped into her throat as she exclaimed, "Oh come on!"

The wall had formed into a hand and had reached out to grab a hold of the rope. Without another thought, she grabbed the clamp and released the line. Her body slid down quickly. When she reached the hand, she released the rope and jumped to the ground. Before it had a chance to grab her, she was already on the floor. Dejected, the hand melded back into the wall.

Haydeez landed on the floor with a not so nimble thud. "Not as graceful as I'd hoped," she grumbled to herself. "Kinda glad I was alone this time." She grunted as she tried to stand. A twinge of pain shot up her leg and a new wound had appeared on her arm. Pushing the throbbing and stabbing pains aside, she forced herself to stand.

Bits of gravel rained down on her. She looked up and barely avoided the pair of hands that reached out to grab her. Her stomach had jumped up into her throat but fell back down quickly as she regained her composure.

She rolled and jumped back up to her feet. She ran towards the exit and skidded to a halt. Blocking her path was a stone creature. It did not match the hands that had tried to grab her but still had an intimidating presence. Compared to Haydeez with her petite figure, the creature stood a good three feet over her.

"Seriously? A stone golem? I really should've seen this coming," she scolded herself as she shook her head. Her arms dropped to her sides as she sighed. "It's like Harrison Ford not knowing the swap wouldn't work, right?" she said to the creature. "The ball's still coming." She scoffed as she shook her head. "You have no idea what I'm talking about."

The creature watched every move she made, waiting for her to try to escape again. It was placed here to protect the piece and now someone had it.

Haydeez mentally judged her chances of making it out without a fight. Based on the size of the golem and the fact that it lived in the tower, she knew she had no chance and would probably have to trick it to get out alive. She sighed, resigned to the inevitable, and said, "Alright, Pebbles, let's dance."

The golem stood in front of the doorway waiting for Haydeez to make a move. She knew she could not just hit it or she would leave with a busted hand, if she left at all. She had to avoid it and hope for an opening to get to the door. The creature took a step towards her. She touched the pocket with the figure, making sure it was still secure.

The creature caught Haydeez off guard when it charged her. It moved faster than she believed possible for something made of living stone. Her heart caught in her throat as she almost did not get out of the way in time.

Haydeez spun around and kicked, trying to throw it off balance. Her soft soled moccasin hit the solid stone of the golem's back and she whimpered a little. "Ok, mistake," she said as she tried to shake it off. Her foot stung but it was something she could handle. She hopped up and down and waited for the golem to turn.

Her jaw dropped as she watched the creature's face push through the back of its head. "Unfair!" she shouted and made a run for the door.

The creature raced towards her. It slammed into her, throwing her petite body against the nearest wall. She hit with a thud and a grunt. Her body smacked into the floor and she could already feel the bruises forming. She paused on the floor, trying to catch her breath. Starbursts filled her vision as she tried to see where her assailant was.

About twenty feet away, the golem stood watching and waiting. Then something occurred to her: As long as she did not try to leave, it left her alone. As soon as she tried to run for the exit, it raced after her with that unnatural speed and trapped her. It had her cornered. She had to think. If she could make it believe she was leaving the bird, she could race for the door and possibly make it safely out of here. She needed to outsmart the rock.

Many long moments passed as she sat on the floor of the tower and tried to figure out how to get out of this mess. She pulled her bag over and was digging around inside. Disappointment and discouragement began to set in as the minutes passed. Nothing in her bag came even remotely close to the bird figure. She started to think that she would not get out of there, at least not with the owl.

Just then, her heart skipped a beat as her fingers brushed over something small in the very bottom of the bag. Hidden under her equipment was the owl from before. The little fake bird was like a beacon on a foggy night. She felt in her side pocket to make sure she had not put it in the bag and just forgot but there it was, warm as ever, pressed against her ribs. She smiled to herself, a renewed strength entered her body.

Keeping the fake in the palm of one hand, she tossed her bag over her other shoulder and stood up. A feeling of calm rippled through her body as she stared down the golem and took a step.

The stone creature took a step towards her, its eyes narrowed. It let out a low rumble that sounded more like a force of nature than a growl. It lifted its arms and took another step.

Haydeez lifted her hand to show the creature what she had. It stopped; its eyes moved from the owl to her face and back again. It did not know which was more important, the figure or the person trying to take it. Confusion passed through its consciousness.

Haydeez smiled, an evil light glinting in her eyes. "What's it gonna be, Pebbles? Me, or the pretty bird?" She took another step forward and waved the owl in front of the creature. "What do you want more?" She taunted the creature.

It followed the figure like a dog eyeing a treat. Once she felt the creature was hooked, she stopped and yelled, "Fetch!" Her voice echoed off the walls as the figure flew from her fingers. It landed across the building on the other side of the tower.

The creature took off after it. Haydeez did not wait around and did not look back. She raced for the door, leaving the golem with its prize. It reached the figure lying on the floor and called up the stone to its fingertips. It picked up the delicate figure in its bulky fingers and paused.

A low rumble began under the tower. The creature crumbled the fake figure into sawdust and splinters and turned to the entrance.

Haydeez was already outside racing to the car when the rumbling began. "Don't turn around. Just keep running," she said to herself between breaths. "It's just pissed off. Just keep running." She tripped as the ground began to bounce beneath her feet and her body tumbled down the hill. She stopped with a grunt and could not help but look back the way she had come. Her breath caught in her throat and her eyes grew wide.

The tower was shifting. Stone ground against stone as arms sprouted from the sides and a head emerged. It pulled itself upright out of the ground and stretched tall in the early afternoon light. All of the golem's focus was on Haydeez. There was no place to hide.

Haydeez scrambled to her feet and began running again, her pack bouncing against her back. "This is absolutely insane!" she shouted. The ground shook again as the giant golem took a step. She could feel everything inside crawling into her stomach and trying to come out of her mouth.

A loud roar sounded behind her as a boulder hit to her left. Dirt and grass sprayed at least ten feet into the air and showered down around her. She spit dust and grass out of her face and pushed her legs faster. The creature tossed another boulder like it was as light as a piece of crumbled paper. It missed Haydeez much like the first. The creature howled in anger.

Haydeez reached the car and practically ripped off the door trying to get inside. She threw her bag on the passenger's seat and jammed the key in the ignition.

Another boulder crashed down outside her window and sprayed debris against the car. The sound of the rock smacking into the pavement and gravel hitting her window made her jump. The ignition roared to life. Haydeez slammed the car in gear and hit the gas. The creature was down the hill and making its way towards her. The larger it was, the slower it seemed to move. This was only helpful before it started hurling chunks of itself at her. Now all she could do was hope that it could not outrun her car.

With her heart threatening to escape from its home, she shifted to drive and pressed the pedal to the floor. The tires squealed in protest. A boulder slammed down where her back tires had just been. "Please go faster!" she yelled at the little car.

She passed the entrance to the park and the boulders stopped. Everything grew eerily quiet and the ground stopped vibrating. The only noise was the soft hum of the rental car and the persistent thud of her beating heart. She slowed down and pulled off to the side of the road. All she could see was the creature standing in the field.

The guardian golem began to crumble. Huge chunks hit the dirt beneath its feet. She watched as piece after piece fell like it had been hit with cannon balls. With one last whimper of anger, the final piece fell to the ground until all that was left was a broken pile of stone. The tower looked like it had been under attack and lost the battle.

Haydeez realized that she had been holding her breath and let it out. After taking a few deep breaths, she reached for her phone. She had not realized how late it actually was. It was coming up on lunch and she had not heard from Linx yet. She looked at her phone. "No signal. Figures," she mumbled. "I'll just call him when I get to the hotel."

With the mess she just left behind, she knew it was best if she disappeared quickly. It would be difficult to explain why she destroyed the tower and right now her brain could barely remember how to drive properly. She turned off her phone to save the battery and headed back to the hotel leaving the crumbled golem in the field behind her.

Chapter 19

Haydeez walked out to her car. She reached into her pocket, pulled out her phone and clicked it on. She stopped to grab something to eat before she headed back to the hotel. The familiar ring sounded, telling her everything was loaded and she had a signal. Before she could lift her hand to dial, her phone beeped. There was a text. A second later, there was another beep telling her she had a voicemail.

The text said that Linx had gotten to the pub and was going to investigate. *Good* she thought to herself. When she checked her voicemail, it said she had four messages. She listened to the first three with no expression. The first one said that Linx had the fish. The next one seemed a little more urgent. The third was Linx yelling into the phone about driving for 18 hours today and something about being used. She could not understand it completely. She hung up before the last message started and called Linx.

"It's about bloody time! What the hell, Haydeez?"

She unlocked the car and opened the door. "And a happy hello to you too. So, you got the fish," she said.

"The fish!" Linx yelled. "That's what you ask about. No, 'are you alright?' or 'sorry you were shot at in your injured state and all'. Bloody hell!"

Haydeez sighed in annoyance as she sat down. "I figured you were alright since you answered. But, since you brought it up, fine. Sorry, you were shot at. By the way, I'm fine too, since you asked and all. No, I wasn't shot at but I did have to avoid being flattened by boulders. Yea, I said boulders."

"What the..." Linx started to ask but was cut off.

"I wasn't done. The owl was guarded by a rock golem." She closed the door and started the engine. "The tower came to life and didn't want to let me go. It hurled chunks of itself at me. Did you hear me? Chunks of stone, bigger than me, flying through the air trying to smear me on the ground.

Sound like fun? Not really. I barely got away. The only positive part is that once the owl left the property, the golem crumbled. So, at least it's not still chasing me. I could've been a bloody mess in the dirt and you'd be left to finish this crap yourself. So, if anyone has something to complain about it's me. Now if we're done with your little bitch fit, perhaps we can figure out the next move." She pulled out of the parking lot and began to head for the hotel.

Linx was quiet for a moment. When he spoke the words were quiet. "Yes, I have the fish. It wasn't really too heavily guarded, just a bunch of humans in a pub," He mumbled and cleared his throat. "I've been well over the limit since I left. I should only be about 2 hours out."

Haydeez sighed. "Then I'll see you when you get here." She hung up before Linx had a chance to say anything.

• • • • •

The phone went dead and Linx just stared out the windshield. "She's going to hand me a new one when I get back," he said to himself. "What the hell is wrong with me? But how was I supposed to know the tower was guarded by a golem? She probably hates me now. I'd hate me too. I guess I did kind of freak out over nothing. Great, how am I going to fix this?" He watched the road, trying to figure out what to say.

Chapter 20

Linx pulled up to the hotel and turned off the engine. Silence closed in like a predator, quick and fierce. He did not want to get out of the car but knew that he had to soon.

He picked up the plaque and opened the door. Before he walked away he remembered that he had not checked for bullet holes. With a wince he walked around the car expecting to see holes peppering the trunk. When he reached the back, he perked up. "No holes. I'm a bloody fantastic driver. Or they were just a lousy shot," he said to himself. "Well then. No harm done." He walked inside.

As he opened the door to the room, he heard, "Food's in the mini. I didn't know how long you'd actually be since you drive like a scared old lady most of the time. So I just got you something cold."

Haydeez sat at her table and wrote something. She looked up. "Plus we have somewhere we have to be. You're going to have to eat in the car." She tore a piece of paper off the notepad and stood up. "This was on the door when I got back. Don't worry. It's not far and I just need you to stay with the car."

Linx walked towards Haydeez. "Look I'm sorry. I…"

"If you start talking, it had better be to tell me you have to go to the bathroom before we leave. If not, shut up. We've got work to do and I don't have time for little girl, mushy crap." She started to walk to the door. "Grab your food and meet me outside. I've already got the car packed up."

Linx walked to the back. "Right. I do have to use the loo now that you mentioned it."

Haydeez just smirked.

•   •   •   •   •

Linx munched on a cold Reuben while Haydeez took the wheel. He read the note over and over and still could not believe it. "So she just wants us to pop down and have a little chat?"

After about fifteen minutes they pulled off the main road and started down a secluded dirt road. Hills tumbled past as the sun moved further west.

"So what are we looking for?" Linx asked. "We're out in the middle of nowhere. You're not looking for a place to hide my body are you?" he laughed.

"Oh please. I've got more than enough property for that back home. And I've always wanted a pig." She looked over, an expression of calm eerily floated through her eyes. "They eat anything." She turned back to the path and remained silent.

Linx glanced over and slowly gripped the door handle.

A smile spread quietly across her lips, eyes remained straight ahead. "Relax. I can't break in a new sidekick, bring them up to speed, and make them comfortable before Pandora destroys the world. It took how long for you to get used to me."

"Hell, you still scare the life out of me. I can only imagine what someone new would think of you," he said.

"I scare you because you see what I can do, what I can fight, and you've lived through it with me," Haydeez said.

Linx scoffed. With a laugh he said, "You scare me because you could knock the sh..." he stopped. His mouth dropped open and his eyes grew wide.

Haydeez stopped the car at the top of a hill overlooking a little valley. The valley looked like something out of a twisted Christmas movie. The ground and surrounding trees were covered in frost. Ice crystals spiked up from the earth like the teeth of some giant monster. Animals were half trapped, frozen in place, with a look of sheer terror.

In the middle of it all was a little girl. She sat patiently on a tree stump with a man behind her. Her delicate hands clasped loosely in her lap, a smile on her lips.

"Right. I'll stay with the car," Linx said. "You can handle the creepy little girl right?"

Haydeez turned to Linx and smirked. "Afraid she's coming for you?" She hit the button to unlock the trunk. "Of course I can." She got out of the car and moved to the rear.

When she opened the trunk, her shot gun glistened proudly on top of a pile of other weapons. She picked it up and put it in its holster.

"Don't you think you're going a little light today, love?" Linx asked. He closed the passenger door.

"I'm a woman. She's the destroyer of *man*," she answered matter-of-factly.

Linx paused for a moment. "Are you sure you want to do this on your own? I mean, this is Pandora." He came around the back of the car. He scratched his arm and took the keys.

"You offering to help? Sure, why don't you take the bow and arrows and... no that's not going to work, is it? Well maybe you could grab the shot gun." She glanced at his shoulder. "Really, Linx. I'll be fine. I don't think I need back up." Her eyes fell on the deer trapped in a block of ice, forever frozen in terror. She could almost feel the cries for help as they slowly slipped into unconsciousness. She started to walk towards the valley. "Stay with the car. I'll be right back."

Linx walked to the driver's side and climbed inside. He watched Haydeez walk away and touched his arm. "Well I just feel ruddy useless," he mumbled. He continued to watch her walk away and, for the second time today, place her life in danger. "Useless."

"Just a child," she mumbled as she got a little closer.

Pandora bounced in her seat. "I told you she would come, daddy," she said as she looked back at the man behind her.

Haydeez walked slowly with her hand near her shotgun. "You must be Eve." Something did not feel right.

Pandora giggled. "Your friend is welcome to join us. There will be no fighting between us today," she said.

Haydeez looked up and motioned to Linx to join her.

"Let us also not pretend that your weapons will actually harm me," Pandora said as she nodded to the shot gun. She looked up at the man behind her and giggled again. "It is so funny that she thinks it will matter." She turned to face Haydeez again and said, "I know what you want." She smiled coyly as she twirled a curl around her finger. "And I know where to find it," she taunted.

Haydeez looked at the little girl. "If you know what we want, then you know we need to stop you."

Pandora's laugh twinkled through the air. It bounced off the large shards of ice all around them. "I would be hurt if you did not try. But remember, I am here for the downfall of man. You have nothing to fear from me, Haydeez."

"Oi! I'm right here!" Linx shouted.

"Hush male mortal. This does not concern you," Pandora said. Her eyes never left Haydeez. "This is for us immortal females to discuss," she said as a wicked smile spread across her lips.

Haydeez furrowed her brow. "Immortals? I'm not immortal."

"Whatever you choose to call it, dear." She touched her finger to her lips. "Speaking of immortals, you really should start your search for that god. He will find it first and then what will you do?"

Haydeez glanced at Linx and asked, "You know where he is?"

Pandora laughed. "Of course not. The Christians have hidden all of them from my view. They were very thorough with that. Sadly, even my father is lost to me. However, I have narrowed my search. I believe I know the general area in which to find him. But, if you do not find him soon, the Alpha will. His intentions, and I believe you will agree, are less than noble." A knowing smile crept across her lips and erased the last traces of the child's innocence.

Haydeez shook her head. There was too much information and too many questions. She was well beyond confused now. "All of them? What are you talking about?"

Pandora laughed once more. "I knew you would be a worthy opponent. You desire knowledge more than I want to destroy man," she began. "The other gods of course. Many long years ago a new god came to town. He was not nearly as powerful as the other, older gods but he was crafty. He had a small group of followers. They were ready for a change. They had been denied by their gods and wanted to show them the anger they felt." She stopped and met Haydeez's gaze. "So they joined the new god."

"So the stories are true," Haydeez said matter-of-factly. "The gods were all trapped. But why are you telling me all this?" Haydeez asked. Her eyes followed every move Pandora made.

"Such impatience. We have plenty of time, child." She crossed her feet at the ankles and placed her hands in her lap. "The new god made a deal with his followers: You make me the most powerful and you will spend eternity in paradise. To be the most powerful, you must have the most followers. How could they say 'no'? No matter what he said, they did as they were told. Finally, he realized that he would never be the most powerful as long as all the other gods were still around."

"He had them killed? I thought you can't kill a god," Linx blurted.

"If I have to tell you again, boy," she snapped as she looked straight into Linx's eyes. Disgust bubbled to the surface and flooded her vision. "I'll make you my new daddy." She cocked her head slightly as a wicked grin crossed her tiny pink lips.

Linx took a step back and looked away.

"Now where was I? Oh yes, the new god charged his original followers with one final task. The older gods could not be destroyed. As long as they had followers, they would survive. But, cut them off from their worship..." she turned her gaze back to Haydeez. "They slowly faded away.

"While I enjoy destruction and torture as much as the next, this new god was walking a thin line. He had to act fast lest the others discover his plan." She kicked her tiny black shoes back and forth. "He charged his followers with the capture and containment of each and every god of every other pantheon. He was afraid of the others and he knew that they would come for him if he did not move quickly.

"The other gods were arrogant and believed that nothing as simple as a mere human could harm them. They gladly walked into the traps thinking that they would easily escape. But they did not. The new god had given them the means to contain each and every being. One at a time, the followers went around trapping the gods, cutting them off, creating a barrier between the gods and their worshipers."

Haydeez shook her head again as she tried to take everything in. "Ok, but this doesn't explain why you're telling me all this. Why would you help me stop you? I don't get it."

"Silly, how can we play a game if you do not know all the rules? To be fair, you must know your enemy to have a chance to win. Of course you will not win but I must at least give you a chance." Pandora put her hand over her lips and giggled.

Haydeez thought for a moment. "Wait, you said you knew where it was. I need to find Cernunnous. But then you said you don't know where he is. How am I supposed to believe anything you say?" she asked.

Pandora held Haydeez's gaze as she giggled again. "That is not what you seek." Her eyes sparkled. "The stag. You still need the final relic. Without it, you will not be able to free the god from his prison."

"Where is it?" Haydeez demanded, her fingers clenched into fists.

Pandora reached for her "daddy", took his hand, and hugged it. A barely audible groan sat in the back of the man's throat. She had turned a normal, loving gesture into something grotesque. "It is in the last place you would even think to look."

"No more jokes. You said you wanted to be fair."

She glared at Haydeez, eyes burned with anger. "Your impulsiveness will get you killed one day, Haydeez." Her voice hissed slightly. She regained her composure and continued. "It is with him. He wears it like a pendant, like a symbol of power and protection. The Alpha holds the final piece to your puzzle. Find him and you can free the god." Pandora swung her arms happily.

Haydeez and Linx watched the display, sickened by the contamination of a pure and innocent soul. She looked at Linx for a moment as confusion once again crossed her face.

"Ok, so where is he and how do I get the stag?" Haydeez asked.

"No, no, no. Silly Haydeez. You cannot have the answers all at once." She giggled. "You have to wait a little while to get the rest. After all, we are playing a game, remember? If I show you all my cards now, how will I beat you?" She giggled again.

"Don't worry. You won't win," Haydeez said matter-of-factly. "It's ok to share your whole plan with us right here and now. In fact, why don't you just give up and go away."

"Fine by me," Pandora said. She took hold of her "daddy's" hand, waved her dainty fingers good-bye, and disappeared.

Linx stood dumbstruck while Haydeez just stared at an empty field.

Chapter 21

"What the hell was that all about?" Linx yelled.

Haydeez began walking back to the car. Linx had to race to keep up with her. "This is a game to her. She's throwing around her power because she's not afraid. She wanted me here so she could tell me her little plan and then she could flaunt it in my face. If she wins, it's over. She gets what she wants. If she loses, she gets to try again another time. She knows we can't destroy her. So, no matter what," she stopped and locked eyes with Linx who almost walked right into her. "She wins." With a turn, she was on the move again.

"So what? We give up now?" Linx asked as he began walking again.

Haydeez laughed so hard she almost tripped. "Give up? Please! Do you even know me, Linx?" They walked up the hill to the car. "We stop her just like we always do. Who cares if she can try again another time? The point is: we need to stop her this time. We figure all this out and then we stop her. If something happens after this, it doesn't matter." She made a gesture for the keys.

Linx tossed them to her. "Right. We just stop her. Good plan."

She opened the trunk and placed her shotgun inside. "Don't be stupid. That's not the plan. That's just the outcome. We work out the 'how' later." She closed the trunk. "We know she's got no problem releasing all kinds of creatures onto the world for her little game." She unlocked the doors.

"You seem unnaturally calm. We have to stop a creature from legend who is attempting to cause the end of the world and you're acting like we're just out of tea." He climbed in the passenger's seat and closed the door.

Haydeez paused. He was right. Over the last few weeks, so much had happened. She had lost her cool on so many occasions *but* now. She was calm. Her head was focused. She had handled many different monsters and not once did she ever fear that she would not see tomorrow.

Now there was the very real possibility that her world, Linx's world, everyone's world would come to an end.

Linx knocked on the inside of the driver's window.

Haydeez opened the door and said, "Sorry. Lost in thought." She sat down and closed the door.

"By the way, did you smell that? Something in that field smelled dead," Linx said.

"I think it was daddy. Did you notice that the curator was no longer with her? It's like she dropped him and got a new one," Haydeez said, confused. "I bet she's sucking the life out of them to keep her spirit in that little girl's body."

Linx shuddered. "It looked like his skin was starting to peel off too," he added.

For a moment, there was silence. As Haydeez started the car, Linx asked, "What do you think she meant by 'immortal'?"

"I have no idea. I'm not immortal. Aren't immortals just always there or they come out like an adult or something?" she asked. "I had a childhood. Granted I have no idea who my real parents are but then again a lot of kids go through that. I mean, I was raised by Joseph and he trained me to be a hunter. Whatever Pandora thinks I am, immortal certainly isn't right."

"Sure a lot of kids don't know who their parents are but how many of those kids play with knives or learn how to shoot a shotgun for a living? And how many hunt monsters every day?" Linx asked.

Haydeez shifted the car into gear. "I don't have percentages but I'm sure they fight monsters in their own way," she said with an awkward smile.

Linx shook his head and chuckled. "Right, I'm sure they do. But I highly doubt their monsters are trying to bring about the destruction of mankind."

Haydeez turned the car around and began to head back towards Bristol. "Are you sure? I mean, I can't possibly be the only one out there fighting to save the world, right? There's got to be other kids that want to be heroes and stuff," she said with a smile. "Otherwise, how would I have found you?"

"There's a difference between 'superhero' and what we do, love," Linx said.

They began to discuss the differences all the way to the hotel.

•   •   •   •   •

Pandora stood in the field cloaked in a veil of illusion. She was completely invisible to Haydeez and Linx. She watched as the pair walked back to the car and discussed the necessity of stopping her.

She giggled. "This is fun, daddy. I knew she would play my game. The harder she tries, the stronger I get. I cannot wait until she releases the god of the Hunt. Everything is working out just the way I want." She hopped up and down with joy. "This will be so much fun!"

She placed a delicate hand over her mouth and added with a tiny gasp, "We should see how our other player is doing. After all, we cannot finish this level of the game without him. Come on, daddy. We need to go," she said eagerly as she tugged on the man's arm.

He started walking without a word. His eyes fixed forward, staring at nothing in particular.

Pandora skipped along as they left the now empty field, happy in the knowledge that things were moving along exactly as planned. "They are so predictable, daddy," she said with a little giggle.

Chapter 22

Gavin surveyed his pack. Ninety percent of the people before him were males. Many of them his Loup Garou remembered from before and he could feel their strength. The others were a mixture of females and weaker males. They had stopped to hunt and eat and almost all of the remaining ten percent sat on the ground breathing heavily or were on the verge of passing out from exertion.

He looked at his pack; large, strong, powerful creatures ready for battle. Then there were the new recruits; weak, small, and afraid. He was disgusted. Why should he care about these inferior creatures? Why should he take them along and consider them his equals when they are clearly subservient. They will not last. It is through his will alone that they had made it this far. *That stops now*, he thought to himself.

He stood and walked toward his pack, revulsion in his mouth, fueled his movements.

He was about to speak when he heard a voice. "What do you intend to do, Gavin?"

He spun around. Nobody had ever snuck up on him. He glared at the source of the voice. Before he moved to attack, he paused. "You," he snarled. "You've come for more payment?"

Pandora walked out of the trees with her daddy's hand in hers. The silver ribbons in her hair sparkled in the moon light. Her curls bobbed slightly as she bounced up to Gavin. "No, silly. I came to see how you were doing. I gave you a very tough task and thought I should stop to see you. Such a task could take its toll on a lesser creature," she said in a mocking tone, complete with a condescending smile.

"Then you've wasted a trip. I'm obviously not a lesser creature and as such it wouldn't be 'taking its toll' on me." Gavin wiped a tiny line of saliva from the corner of his mouth. Ever since the creature returned, he felt more anger than he ever had.

"How sad," Pandora said. "Have you located the god of the Hunt yet? After all, that is all that I have asked of you, right? Locate and destroy the Green Man. It is a simple task for one with your..." she paused. "Unique abilities." She smiled an innocent grin.

Gavin began to growl deep within his chest. "As I've said, I'll find and destroy my former 'Master' not because you desire it. But because I desire it, I deserve it." His muscles tensed. He knew Pandora tried to bait him. He would not allow a female, immortal or not, to belittle him, especially in front of his pack. "I have everything under control. I can feel him. We're getting closer and soon we'll find him and destroy him. Both our problems will be solved," he said with contempt. He flexed his fingers into fists but did not make a move against the child.

Pandora shook her head. "It is not nice to wish harm on those who help you. You would be wise to remember such things, canine." She reached for the golden dial and began realigning images. "If someone were to take offense, they may be inclined to take back a gift." A chilled wind began to swirl around Pandora and Gavin.

Gavin could feel the warmth of the Loup Garou being violently ripped from his soul like it had once before all those years ago. He remembered now what it felt like when he lost a part of him. The angst he felt was more than any living creature could handle. He howled in pain and yelled, "Enough! Enough! You win!" The winds abruptly stopped and the creature retreated further into Gavin, licking its wounded ego. "I apologize for any insult that may have passed between us, verbally or otherwise. The beast is angry and wishes to finish this task once and for all." He looked away from Pandora's eyes. He did not wish to instigate another challenge. He had never felt defeat until now. He did not like it.

Pandora bounced up and down happily. "No harm done. Now you must know that there is someone who wishes to prevent you from completing your task. At this moment, she is collecting pieces that will give her the power to release the Green Man from his prison. Do you know what will happen if he is released, Gavin?"

The creature stirred in Gavin's belly. "If he's released, I've failed." He took the chance and locked eyes with Pandora. "I don't fail." The muscles in his arms twitched with anticipation as he thought of what he wanted to do to this woman should she try to release his master.

"Oh goody!" Pandora exclaimed. "Then you should hurry because she seems very determined to get to him first. Just remember, she is very good. I have seen her fight."

Gavin let out a growl. "Nobody is a better fighter. Nobody's ever bested me. She won't succeed." His body grew warmer; the heat emanated out into the pack. Some of them could withstand the pressure, but not many. Those who were too drained from the travel collapsed to the ground and groaned. The others merely bowed and averted their eyes.

Pandora smiled, her eyes lit up. "Then hurry, Gavin! You cannot let her win. She will need your pendant to release the god. Do not let her have it or you will lose for sure." She pushed him. "Your stag is the final key to release him from his prison," she whispered eagerly.

Gavin's eyes darkened and a low rumble began deep within his body. The creature began to climb to the surface as Gavin spoke. "Then she will die wanting." He let out a howl that caused the weaker pack members to cringe and huddle together on the ground. Goose bumps covered their skin as those who were still human began to change. The power began to ripple throughout the group as each human was forced into the change, pulled to the ground, and had their own beasts ripped to the surface of their skin.

In a voice that barely resembled that of his human side, Gavin said, "With the pulse of the earth itself, I will reach him first and both will become sustenance for my brethren." He stood before Pandora as the Loup Garou, an army of dogs at his heel. "We will feast on the flesh of a god!" he shouted. His pack responded in a chorus of howls. War was declared; bloodshed and death the only ending.

Chapter 23

A knock sounded on the door of room 308. Haydeez called to the person at the door, asking them not to leave. A moment later the lock clicked and the door opened.

"Room service, ma'am," said a man dressed in server's clothing.

"Thanks, I needed something stronger than tap water," Haydeez said. She stood in the open doorway, hair dripping wet, with a fluffy white hotel towel wrapped around her muscular petite frame. A pleasant smile crossed her lips. "You, sir, are a life-saver. Come on in." She stepped aside and motioned the man into the room.

She walked over to one of the double beds and flopped down. As she reached for her wallet, she grabbed a pillow with her other hand. "Wake up," she said quietly. With a swift movement, she smacked a sleeping Linx in the back of the head with the pillow. He grunted something she could not understand. She thumped him again.

"Ok. Ok. I'm up." He rolled over and pushed himself up with his good arm, the sheet sliding off his bare shoulders and bunching in his lap. He went to scratch his arm but stopped as has fingers brushed the cast.

Haydeez handed the man a tip. He responded with, "Thank you, ma'am and should you need anything else this evening, or any other time during your stay here, I will be happy to assist you. Please do not hesitate to ask." His hands shook slightly.

"Ok, thanks," she said.

He backed out the door with and eager smile. "Have a wonderful evening, ma'am," he said before closing the door.

Linx yawned. "How much did you give him?" he asked.

Haydeez shrugged. "Don't know. Didn't look. Why?"

"Because I think he loves you now," Linx scratched his head and slid off the bed. He walked over to the cart and grabbed a bottle of Tennets. After trying unsuccessfully to open it himself, he walked over to Haydeez in his Warlock pajama pants and asked, "Would you mind?" He handed her the bottle.

She took the bottle and popped the cap. "And you thought I would need you," she joked. Before she handed it back, she pretended to take a drink. "Oh did you want this back?" she asked with a smirk.

He grabbed for the bottle and she jerked it back. "Ha ha so funny. Keep away from the guy who can only grab with one hand. You're such a child." Haydeez stuck out her tongue. "My mistake. That makes you an adult," he said sarcastically.

She laughed. "It does. Don't be jealous because I'm so much more mature than you." She licked the top of the bottle and then handed it back to him.

He began to laugh as he snatched the bottle. "That's mature?" He shook his head and took a sip. "If that's mature, I think there are a lot of people that don't know how to grow up." He stopped and looked at Haydeez. "Did you just get out of the shower?"

She looked down at the towel and touched her hair. "What the... Well look at that. I think I did." She stuck out her tongue again. "Why?" She stood up and grabbed a bottle of Tennets for herself.

He cleared his throat. "And you're not wearing anything under that are you?"

"No, Linx. I shower in my bathing suit." She rolled her eyes.

Linx took a deep breath and closed his eyes. "Why do you do that to me?" he mumbled. He could sense goose bumps on his arms and his cheeks began to feel hot.

Haydeez began to laugh. "Aw Linx, do I embarrass you with my near nakedness? At least I'm not wearing pajamas from a band that doesn't exist and hasn't existed since the 80s," she taunted him. She grabbed a stack of clothes from a chair near her bed, walked into the bathroom, and closed the door.

"Whoa there, love." Linx turned around and walked to the bathroom door. He leaned against the door frame. "You have obviously never listened to Doro Pesch. She was, and is to this day, the epitome of metal. She's a metal goddess."

"Really, Linx?" Haydeez said from inside the bathroom.

"Yes really. You probably think Lita Ford is the best because she did a song with Ozzy. Well, let me tell you, love. One song with the Ozzman does not a goddess make. When the Ozzman cometh, he's fantasizing about Doro."

"Wow, Linx. That was really horrible. I can't believe you actually said that." Haydeez laughed again as she opened the door.

Linx tensed. "You ok?" Haydeez smirked. "Have I offended your delicate nature, Linx?" she whispered as she brushed past him.

Goose bumps shivered up and down his body and his cheeks began to flush again. His heart was racing and everything inside him grew hot. "Offend isn't the word I'd use," he said, a slight tremble in his voice. He cleared his throat.

Haydeez flopped back on the bed and slid back as she pulled her feet up. "Movie time. We have to clear our heads and relax a little. So, what's it going to be?" She propped herself up on her arms and leaned back slightly. With her legs crossed at the ankles, she added, "Action? Comedy? I'll do anything but that romantic crap right now. Just not in the mood at the moment."

Linx sighed, a feeling of disappointment flooded his body. "Trust me. I know." He shouldered himself off the doorframe and walked over to his bed. He threw himself face down on his pillow and grunted as he landed on his arm. "Wow, that was completely stupid of me," he said. "Whatever you want to watch is fine by me." He turned his head to look at Haydeez.

She smiled eagerly and hopped off the bed to get the movie guide. "Comedy it is," she said.

Linx watched her in her white silk pajamas. She bounced on her toes while she looked through the guide. The material shimmered in the light. The shirt and pants hung loosely and waved slightly with every move she made. Her golden hair fell down past her shoulders. It was still damp from the shower but it danced around her face in spite of the moisture. Her eyes glittered as she turned to him and asked, "Ready?"

She could have done any number of things that would normally destroy the mood and he still would have looked at her for what she was. Haydeez had passion and heart for everything she did. She had trusted him, on more than one occasion, with her life. He could not think of anyone else that had ever done that. She cared very much for him but she made it very clear that she wanted him around in a purely platonic capacity. The problem was he wanted something more. His head told him to let it go but his heart kept saying that there was always a chance. From the moment he had met her, everything about her was enticing and scary at the same time. He obviously knew about the creatures she hunted and knew as much as she did about the people who paid her to do it. What he never understood was what she wanted from life. After asking her once, he got the most round-the-bend answer anyone had ever given. He decided not to ask again. So he remained a friend but never let her forget that he was there and would remain close until she was ready.

But now was not that time. So, taking the hint from his brain for the moment, he smiled and said, "Sure, whenever you're ready, love."

Chapter 24

"Linx," Haydeez mumbled in a sleepy haze. "Do you hear knocking or is that just my head?" she asked slowly.

There was a little movement and Linx poked his head from under his pillow. "If it's your head then someone should tell mine because I hear it too." He pulled the covers off and swung his legs over the side of his bed. He rolled over the side and fell to the floor with a thump. "Ow. I'm ok," he mumbled. "Haydeez, did you move the door?"

Haydeez lifted her head from under the pillow. "Why would I move the door?"

"Because the knocking's coming from right here." He pulled himself up and reached over the side of the bed to tap Haydeez. She rolled over to see where he was looking. Linx pointed to the drawer in the night stand between the beds. "Am I imagining this?"

The knocking continued.

A light clicked on inside Haydeez brain. "Keeglian," she slurred. As she tried to get up, her head swam and she collapsed back on the bed.

"I got this, love. I'm already right here," Linx said. He drew a few symbols with his finger on the drawer, knocked in response and scooted back.

The drawer popped open. "Bloody hell, I hate when I grab a small opening," a voice said from inside the drawer. "Oh well, it *is* open now." A head squeezed up out of the drawer as Keeglian forced his way into the room. It looked a lot harder than it actually was as the magic that created the connection allowed him to fit comfortably through any entrance he chose.

After a moment, he stood in the hotel room staring at Haydeez. "Are you alright?" he asked. "You look positively dreadful."

Haydeez pressed the heel of her palm against the side of her head and sat up slowly. "Long night trying to take our minds off the situation. The alcohol won but I put up a pretty damn good fight." Her hair was crumpled up on one side. When she moved the blanket aside to stand up, one pant leg was pushed up past her knee to expose a large purple bruise. "Oh hey, look at that. I wonder where that came from." She poked at it and winced slightly. "Hmm, don't remember falling down anywhere or..." She paused and looked around the room. "Oh that's right. I thought the dresser wanted to fight. Wow, how much did I drink last night?" She searched for empty bottles but could only find two. The cart was also missing.

"I vaguely remember calling down for more. They probably took the empties when they brought the new stuff," Linx said. He chuckled. "Guess we took our minds off the problem then, love."

Haydeez started to laugh and then groaned for a moment as the throbbing in her head caused her to reach in desperation for the nearest trash can.

Keeglian rolled his eyes. "You can't possibly think that you're in any condition to go anywhere right now." He sighed. "What would you do without me?" he mumbled as he pulled a little pouch from his pocket. What he pulled out would cause anyone else to cover their mouth and run for the nearest toilet. It had the scent combination of skunk and fresh dirty diaper. "Eat this and you should be fine within a few moments." He handed what looked like a seed to both Haydeez and Linx. Without thinking or questioning they both popped the little stinky seed into their mouths and swallowed.

"Can't possibly make me feel any worse than I do right now," Haydeez said. "What does it do?"

Just as she finished asking the question she turned to stare at Linx. They locked eyes. With a speed they did not know they had, both jumped up and raced for the bathroom. Haydeez made it inside a split second before Linx and slammed the door. He banged on the door and yelled, "You better be bloody quick about it!" He turned to Keeglian. "What the hell did you do to us?"

Keeglian stepped further into the room away from the beds and said, "That smelly little seed will extract all the alcohol from your blood and remove it from your body." He smiled smugly. "It happens very quickly. The body has to get rid it somehow. Hence the rush to the loo." He chuckled. "It's only temporary."

Linx stood in front of the door and hopped up and down like a child. He banged on the door again. "About done in there? You're not the only one here remember. I can only hold it for so long." He cringed, his bladder protesting every second he had to wait.

The lock clicked and Haydeez stepped into the room. She looked completely refreshed, hair in place. The bruise on her knee was also starting to change color quickly. She looked as if the previous night had never happened.

Linx shoved past her and slammed the door. There was a lot of moaning from the closed door. Haydeez laughed. She walked over and sat at the little office area they had set up in the room. It was really just a small desk and a couple chairs. "Are you hungry, Keeglian?" Haydeez asked as she picked up the phone to dial for room service.

"No thank you. I'd just like to discuss what I've found and get back," he responded.

"Let me just get an order in and then you've got my complete attention," Haydeez said.

•　　　•　　　•　　　•　　　•

Haydeez poured a cup of coffee as she listened. "So, you'll probably find the tree in a secluded area. It's possible that it's located on an island. The more secluded the better. They wouldn't want anyone to find it and put the pieces together." Keeglian stood with his hands clasped. "It should be simple enough."

"The problem is that we don't have that last piece. Without it we might as well just go home. We need to find the Alpha and get the piece," Linx said.

Haydeez took a sip of her coffee. "Or we find the tree first, put the other four pieces in place, and wait for the big doggie to get there." She turned to look at Keeglian. "As long as we find it first, we still have a chance."

"That could actually work. Now you just need to find the tree," Keeglian said.

"And you're sure he's in a tree?" Linx asked.

"Of course. It makes complete sense. Being the Lord of the Forest, it would only seem right that he be imprisoned there. Plus, those pieces you found are made of wood. It would be the only logical conclusion," Keeglian said, no smugness or contempt for the question. He just answered matter-of-factly, as if the answer was obvious and he was simply voicing it.

Linx grabbed a cup of coffee and sat on the bed. There was silence in the room and nobody looked at each other. "Right. So we're just going to sit here and wait for him to show up then," Linx said sarcastically. "Fantastic plan. There was a film I wanted to watch anyway." He leaned back and took a sip, cringing at the bitterness. "You order coffee to irritate me, don't you, love?

We're in England. Order tea." She stuck her tongue out at him in response. "Are we really going to start that again?" he joked.

"No, we're not going to just sit here and wait. I was trying to think of where we could start looking for this tree. It's usually best to have an idea of where you're going before you get into your car and start driving," Haydeez said. "So, if you're in such a hurry to get started, where would you propose that we look first, smart guy?" Haydeez leaned back in her chair and crossed her arms.

It was Linx's turn to stick out his tongue now. "Ah, I see we're going the mature route again today. Perhaps later we'll kick each other on the playground and you'll pull my pigtails." She turned to Keeglian. "Do you have any suggestions? Or would you just like to stick your tongue out at me as well?"

Keeglian looked at Haydeez. "If I understood the purpose for sticking out one's tongue, I would still refrain from doing it. As I've said, the more secluded the better. Perhaps you could start looking at the smaller islands in the area."

Linx scoffed. "That's your suggestion? Do you realize how many there are in the area? Do you realize that England itself is an island?" He turned to Haydeez and added, "For this kind of help I could go to a fortune teller. Vague and suggestive. How exactly does that help us?" He crossed his arms and furrowed his brow.

Haydeez sighed. "Look, these little birds and their fish friend give off a kind of energy. That's how I found the owl in the tower. The closer you get to it, the stronger the pulse. If we can find a similar pulse, we can follow it and find the tree. Yes, it'll be difficult but we can't let the Alpha get to it first. If he destroys the tree, he'll kill Cernunnous and for whatever reason, Pandora wants him dead. If she wants something dead, that means we want him alive." She stood up and walked over to her backpack. She pulled out the four pieces and set them on the table.

The wooden figures were still warm to the touch. Haydeez could feel the life flowing through them, pulsing like a beating heart. "So, all we have to do is figure out how to follow the pulse. We need these pieces to feel the tree and follow the line home, sort of like a homing beacon." She sighed again. "Unfortunately, I have no idea how to do that." She stood next to the table staring at the pieces, willing them to show her what she needed to do.

Linx walked over to one of his cases. "A homing beacon, huh. Beacons I can work with, love. It might take me a little while but, well, you know."

"You can find the trail?" Haydeez asked.

"Through the pulse of those pieces, I can find the tree," Linx said triumphantly. He was like a kid who had just shown his parents a picture he had drawn. Haydeez was like a mom trying to decipher the image without asking what it was and hurting the child's feelings. Linx looked back and forth between Keeglian and Haydeez. "What?" he asked incredulously. "Seriously, I know what I'm doing." He dug through his bag and pulled out a little piece of equipment. "Ha! I knew I'd need this for something." He grinned again as he showed off his toy. He reached for one of the pieces and picked it up.

"What is that?" Haydeez asked.

"You'll see," Linx said with a wink.

Haydeez watched without another word. She had learned over the years that if Linx said he could do something and it involved technology in any way, he could probably do it. She watched his excitement and let him have his moment. He deserved it.

After a few minutes of nothing, the device began to chirp and flash, just like a signal flare.

"What did you just do?" Haydeez finally asked.

Linx showed her the screen. The device resembled a mixture of a smart phone and grocery store scanner. "I modified a few things and reworked them to make my little friend here. It scans something and uploads the energy signature into the minicomputer inside and then tells me what I want to know." He was so proud he could hardly contain it. "The slower the chirp, the further away we are. The faster, well you know how it works." He looked at the screen again. "It looks like we have to go that way," he said as he pointed in a northern direction. The problem with the machine was that it did not tell them how far away they had to go, just the general direction, but it was a start.

Haydeez watched the little dot for a moment. "So you're Cernunnous," she said quietly. "We'll see you in a bit my friend. We've got some traveling to do." She looked up and said, "Let's pack up and head out then. Looks like we'll be on the road a lot today."

Chapter 25

The morning sun did nothing to drag the chill from the pack as they trekked across an open field. Their collective breath came in bursts of white puffs. The Alpha tried to keep them as far from the cities as possible. He hated the smell of humans. In a city, they were packed so tightly together that their scents combined into floating balls of invisible clouds filled with the most horrid stench he could imagine. He breathed in the fresh crisp air and filled his lungs till they could burst. Anything that could not survive in the wild did not deserve to live, let alone thrive. After all the years he was forced to live among them, he should have gained a little compassion for humans, but he had not gained anything except more hatred and contempt.

During his time in Cernunnous's pack, he came to realization that he had no use for humans, especially females. He did not need to procreate. To make new pack members, all he had to do was take over a new town and assimilate them into the pack.

His body reveled in the freedom he would soon taste. He could almost feel his leash loosen the closer they got to Cernunnous. His muscles tingled and nerves stood at attention. The longer he stayed as the Alpha, the closer their minds were to becoming one. The beast began to squash every last bit of human thought left in Gavin's mind. Soon there would be nothing left but the desires of the creature.

He was so lost in thought that he did not notice someone watched them. Granted the humans who watched him and his pack were far away and downwind. They hid beneath the shadows of a set of trees off in the distance. Each one had a pair of binoculars and a notepad. The only sound they made was when one scratched a little note on the paper. For fear of being discovered, neither spoke a single word. They both knew that he would hear them, even this far away. Once the Alpha and his pack was out of sight, they could discuss what they saw.

With baited breath, they watched as the pack headed north. Over one hundred dogs of all different colors and sizes followed the Alpha as his long canine legs propelled him closer to his goal.

Once the dogs were out of sight of even the binoculars, the two men let out the breath they had been holding. One of the men, a blonde wearing a sweatshirt and jeans sat back on his feet and said, "Please tell me you saw that too. Because if you didn't, I really need to quit drinking." He exhaled audibly. He realized that all his muscles had been tensed and he had to consciously release them. "That thing's huge. How are we supposed to take him down with all those dogs around him? We'll be eaten in minutes." He looked to his companion.

An older man looked back as he ran his fingers through his greying hair. He breathed in and let it out slowly before he spoke. "That thing shouldn't be here. I don't know how it got out but you know what happens if it stays out, right?" he asked, concern and fear crossing his face. "We've gotta let the Council know. They'll know how to deal with it." He collected his things and moved to a crouched position. "We may not see him anymore, but there's still a chance he can see us. Stay low and get back to the car. The sooner we get to the Council, the sooner we don't have to worry about him anymore. Come on," he said, his voice low. He could feel the fear bubbling up and refused to let it escape. If he could hold it back, maybe he could keep the Alpha from smelling him and coming back to take care of him. He could only hope that the breeze did not change direction.

Crouched low, he made his way back to the car they had parked about a half mile away. The younger man followed close behind, trying to stay hidden. They had to uncover their vehicle from all the branches and loose brush they had covered it with before they could get inside to the safety.

Once they were in the car, they both breathed a sigh of relief as the engine purred to life.

•   •   •   •   •

By the time the two men reached their destination, the sun had begun to set and shadows stretched out across the courtyard. They pulled up to the front door and two armed guards stepped up to the car. Several more guards looked out onto the property to ensure the car was not followed. Every sentry on the property was tense and ready to strike, their guns in hand, eyes alert. Muscles twitched as they waited for the men to exit the vehicle.

The two men stepped out of the car, both looked around nervously. One held the pads with all their findings. The other wiped sweat from his brow, eyes darting around. The guards rushed them inside without a word.

The party walked down the entry hallway as quickly as they could without running. The younger man clutched the papers tightly.

They came up to a large set of wooden doors. Each guard slid a door quietly to either side. Then the two men hurried into the room.

A group of seven men were gathered around a large rectangular oak table. Some were old men, hair greying or completely bald, wrinkles, and a sour expression. The others were younger, hair slicked back or cropped short military style. The only common thread between them was that they all wore the same grey suit with the same talisman hanging from a deep purple silk sash around their respective necks. Each man sat quietly awaiting the other two to arrive, hands clasped together on the table. The scene looked like a living painting, so perfectly still except for the occasional rise and fall of someone's chest as they breathed.

The moment the doors closed, the man at the head of the table spoke. "You've asked us to convene to discuss an issue. Let's not waste any time here as our time is much more valuable than you know. What seems to be the problem, gentlemen?" He leaned back in his chair and placed his hands on his lap. The smooth leather didn't squeak when he moved. His weathered features remained tranquil, no emotion behind his eyes.

The younger of the two men spoke first. "The Council asked us to keep them informed if we find something that shouldn't be. Well, not only have we found something but we also think it's going to cause an even bigger problem." His hands were shaking and his face was covered in sweat. He didn't want to be the one to bring this news to the Council but that didn't matter. He was here now and they had to know so they could fix it. Everyone and everything was in danger now.

One of the other men at the table spoke with a heavy Italian accent. "If you have news to share, I would suggest you spit it out, boy. We're very busy and you're wasting time," he snapped. His black hair was slicked back and looked as hard as a helmet. His dark eyes filled with contempt. He hated being interrupted by these supposed 'sightings'. The man at the head of the table lifted his left hand to silence the other council member. "My apologies, Venerated One," he bowed his head slightly in reverence to the elder man.

The young man swallowed hard and took a shaky breath. He looked to his companion for support.

The other man rolled his eyes and took the notepad. He cleared his throat. "Council members, I'd hoped to never have to bring you this news but it appears that somehow the Loup Garou was released. Our investigation shows that the god is still trapped but it looks like the Loup Garou and the god's pack are headed in the right direction. According to our count, there are more dogs than before he was trapped. We didn't think they could recruit anymore but apparently they could. We come here today seeking your expert advice in how to deal with this situation." He bowed his head and waited patiently for a response. In this building he knew his safety was guaranteed.

The old man spoke with an elegant British accent, but still no signs of any emotion. "Well, gentlemen, we knew this day may come. Now we have to deal with it. The Loup Garou can't make it to the island to release his master. Not to say he physically can't make it there because he and the pack are more than capable of reaching their master. However, it simply isn't an option. So what do we do?" He looked around the table at the other members of the Council, stopping to lock eyes with each man in turn.

The men mumbled and cursed as they all tried to come up with a way to deal with this inconvenience. Each voice carried its own brogue. The seconds dragged on as they spoke for what seemed like hours. All the while, the two messengers stood at the other end of the table, awaiting their orders.

The man who had been silenced by the Venerated One spoke. "As you all are aware, I have a weapon that's constantly at my disposal. Should you all agree to use it, I'll make the call and set everything in motion." He smirked at the group, proud of himself for bringing something useful to the table when all the others could bring was complaints and curses. He patiently waited while they discussed his offer, completely confident that they'd agree with him.

The men went back and forth over whether or not Peter was right. The German did not like to use his weapon so often because he felt it was pointless to pay someone for something you could do yourself. Over the years, he had taken care of many minor problems on his own, without any outside assistance. It was how he was most comfortable.

Another man with grey hair and tanned skin believed it was better to use the weapon than get their own hands dirty. A Slavic voice spoke up. "The world doesn't know who we are. Do we really want to make our existence known? Handling this on our own would definitely bring us to light. We have to be smart about this."

As with most other discussions, they ended up agreeing that the use of Peter's weapon was the best option. The Venerated One turned to Peter and said, "Make the call." He turned to the two messengers and said, "You've done well. The Council is pleased that you've brought us this news so quickly. It's always a pleasure to receive such information swiftly." He looked at one of the other members, an older man of Spanish decent with thick dark hair and eyes that could slice out a man's heart. A look passed between the two and the Spanish man pulled a phone from his pocket. He pressed a few buttons and the doors opened. "Your swift attention to this will be rewarded as well." He nodded at the man that entered.

The messengers turned nervously. The younger man's hands shook slightly. The stranger lifted his hand and fired a shot straight into the younger man's head. With a flick of his hand, he changed directions and fired a single shot into the other man's forehead as well.

The Venerated One nodded. "La Garduna stills holds a place to this day," he said as he smiled his approval to the stranger and the Spanish Council member. Nobody at the table flinched as the two bodies were dragged from the room. The Council returned its focus to the Venerated One who looked to his left and said, "Peter, the call."

Peter smiled respectfully and bowed his head slightly. "Of course, Venerated One. Right away." He pulled out his phone and dialed.

•   •   •   •   •

"I'm not exactly at home right now, Peter. What do you want now?" Haydeez sat in the passenger seat holding the device that Linx made in one hand and her cell phone in the other. She held the phone up to her ear, never taking her eyes from the little blinking dot.

"And how is my favorite little hunter today? Having a bad day?" Peter answered in his typical condescending tone. "I have another job for you."

Haydeez looked confused. "Another job? I'm still working on the first one and, again, I'm not at home." Her voice carried a hint of annoyance. She pulled out a map and started scanning the area for possible destinations.

"Silly little Haydeez," Peter laughed. "I pay your bills. I call you with a job and you do it. That's our arrangement." Peter said, anger filtering through the phone lines. He hated being talked down to and hated it even more when his employees disrespected him.

Haydeez scoffed. "You pay my bills? Listen up, Peter, because this is the last time I'll be saying this. I work for me and nobody else. You want something found, you call me because you're just not willing to get your hands dirty. I'm not your puppet. I'm not your dog. Continue to treat me like that and you'll see exactly how good I am at my job. Now," she paused and pointed to the street ahead. She motioned for Linx to make a right turn.

"If you have something you need me to do, I'll be happy to handle it when I get home. You're not the only one paying me to trek all over the world hunting things. Plenty of people want me."

Linx snickered and whispered, "I do."

Haydeez smirked and elbowed him. "Do we have an understanding, Peter?" She waved Linx into a parking lot.

There was silence for a moment and then Peter cleared his throat. "Of course, Haydeez."

"Good. Now why don't you give me a quick rundown of what you want and when I'm done with this job, I'll be sure to call you back." Haydeez turned to Linx and grinned.

Linx looked at her funny and whispered, "You could've said you were hungry." He shook his head and turned off the car.

She mouthed 'I'll be right in' and waited for Peter to explain his newest predicament and how she could fix it for him.

•　　　•　　　•　　　•　　　•

Linx sat and tapped his menu on the table, his eyes on the wall, and waited for Haydeez to come inside. After about fifteen minutes, Haydeez flopped down in the booth across from Linx with a big smile on her face. "Do I want to know?" he asked cautiously.

"You'll never guess what Peter wants me to hunt down," she said with a smile still on her face.

"The Alpha?"

"No fair. Were you listening?" Haydeez answered with a fake pout. "Anyway, I told him he was damn lucky I was already in this area checking a lead on the other missing trow. He doesn't have to know I was looking for the big bad wolf first. So he's going to pay me to do something I was already working on. Lucky me," she chuckled.

Linx shook his head and laughed. "I don't know how you get so lucky but at least we're on the same side. I'd hate to have you hunting me."

"Afraid you can't hold your own against me?"

"No, I *know* I can't hold my own against you," he corrected her with a laugh. "Besides, I don't hit girls anyway." He took a sip of his drink.

Haydeez laughed. "And that's the only reason I'd beat you huh? I'll remember that." She eyed him with a grin.

Linx looked confused and sat back. "You said you didn't want to train a new assistant remember?" he said as he pretended to be nervous.

"Sidekick and relax. I won't hurt you that bad," she said with an innocent grin.

It was Linx's turn to laugh now. "Right. That innocent look definitely doesn't work on you, love. I know better."

• • • • •

Peter looked at the rest of the Council and said smugly, "She'll be taking care of our little problem. She's in Europe investigating those other little creatures and will be handling both problems at once." He sat back in his chair and crossed his arms, pleased with himself and everything he thought he had done.

"Well done, Peter," the Venerated One said. "And she knows nothing of the god's capture? She knows only that she must destroy the Alpha?" he asked, certain to make it clear that she knew only what was necessary.

Peter bowed his head slightly. "Of course, Venerated One. I would never think to give a weapon more information than where they need to go and what they need to shoot. It's not like she has a mind of her own or anything. She is after all, just a woman." He looked around the table.

Everyone nodded their agreement.

Chapter 26

Haydeez and Linx walked casually out to the car. "He's lucky he's got a hefty checkbook following him. Otherwise, I think I'd have to shoot him on merit." Haydeez laughed. "My ex didn't even talk to me like that and I took his dignity." She shook her head.

Linx stiffened a little at the mention of her ex-husband. If he knew he would not get caught, he would go after the guy himself. After everything her ex put her through, Linx believed that he wanted that man dead even more than Haydeez did. If she asked him to, he would probably go and do it himself. He did not really care that the other man was bigger and more powerful, monetarily speaking of course. Decency and honor always won out for him. It helped knowing that she would never ask him to do it too.

"So how much are they paying this time?" Linx asked.

Haydeez smiled. "There's a five and lots of happy little zeroes."

Linx's eyes widened. "He must be desperate. I wonder why he wants the Alpha gone so badly. I mean, I know why we want him gone but Peter..." he paused. "Do you think he knows about Cernunnous?"

Haydeez stopped, her hand on the door handle. She thought for a moment about what she really knew about Peter, which ended up being very little. He paid her by cash most of the time but always sent an unknown messenger to deliver it. They had never officially met. She had only seen his lackeys and even then it was rare. The only reason she took his money was because the things she hunted were dangerous and needed to be stopped. So why not get paid to do what you were going to do anyway? But she did not really know anything about him. She shook her head and opened the door. "If he does, he's not talking. All he told me was that the Alpha was very dangerous and needed to be stopped. He told me the direction he was going in and a guess of how many dogs he had following him." She sat down and closed the door. "It does seem a little weird that he'd ask me to go after something like this and not have more information on it. He's usually pretty good about getting the details to me first." She stared off in an attempt to get a handle on everything. Something felt a little off inside of her but she could not place it. What she really wanted was to find out more about Peter and the guys he makes his decisions with, but that was not the big issue at the moment.

Linx chuckled. "Maybe he's part of one of those secret societies, like in the movies. Maybe it's like the Illuminati or something."

Haydeez turned to look at Linx with an expression that questioned his sanity and intelligence. She burst out laughing. "I really hope you're not serious. Honestly, could you see me working for the church?" She laughed harder. "Shot gun in one hand, sword in the other. Hello, Father, what would you like me to kill today?"

They shared a good laugh as Linx pulled out of the parking lot and back onto the main road. They almost missed the turn back onto the highway because they were so caught up in their revelry.

•　　　•　　　•　　　•　　　•

A horn blared and high-beams flashed as the little car drifted into the next lane. Linx swerved back into his own lane and smacked himself in the face to make sure he was awake. "Oi! We're stopping for the night." He elbowed Haydeez. Her head rested quietly against the window, the soft light of the tracker barely illuminated her features. She looked so peaceful. Linx elbowed her a little harder to wake her.

Haydeez whipped her arm around and stopped as her wrist touched the skin of his neck. Her eyes flew open. "What?" she yelled. When she realized that she had almost crushed his windpipe, her muscles relaxed and she rubbed her face. "Where are we?" she asked with a yawn.

"Middle of nowhere and we're stopping for the night," he answered with a yawn of his own. "Almost drifted into a truck. I think he was carrying something nasty. All I smell is..." Linx's voice cut off for a moment. He stared off to the right side of the road as he took his foot off the gas. The car began to decelerate. "When was the last time you checked the tracker, love?"

Haydeez stretched. "Huh? Um, I think I fell asleep a couple hours ago. Why?" She looked down. "Stop the car!" she yelled. Her eyes were wide as she looked out the window. "Something's here!" she yelled.

Linx pressed the breaks and pulled off to the shoulder. He shut off the head lights and just left the running lights on as they sat in the cold dark and stared at the empty field to their right, almost empty.

The tiny screen in Haydeez lap showed two little dots now. One was right on top of them and the other was somewhere to the north. As their eyes began to adjust to the dark, they noticed movement in the distance. What looked like a hill from far away, moved slightly. "What is that?" Linx asked. "It can't be water. Even in the dark we'd be able to tell. It's not a car. Too big for that." He squinted and tried to make out shapes.

The dark mass flowed across a ridge in the moonlight. Then, the mass came to an end and they could see only the ground. Haydeez hand whipped around again, this time grabbing Linx by the shirt. "The dogs," she whispered. "It's the dogs. The Alpha is right over there. We've been following him this whole time." She turned around to stare at Linx. "We've been following his trail." Her heart had jumped into her throat and her body grew slightly colder. "I don't know what to do. I thought we were getting closer to the tree but now, I really don't know what to do." Her eyes were wide, not in fear but because she had never found herself in a situation where she could not come up with a plan.

Linx pealed her fingers off his shirt and held her hand. "Take a breath. Relax. He hasn't seen us yet and probably doesn't even know we're here. If we just keep driving, we'll be far away from him and that much closer to the tree. Then, we can figure out what to do. For now, you need to breathe. We'll be fine," Linx squeezed her hand gently with the hope that his words had helped. His heart beat so fast he could not tell if the engine or his body vibrated more. He took his own advice and took a deep breath and let it out slowly.

Haydeez let out a breath she had held and relaxed her hand. She could feel a cold sweat beading up on her face and her neck. Even in the warmth of the car's heater, her skin felt like ice. Slowly, the warmth began to return to her arms and she calmed a bit more. "I hadn't expected to see him right now. I truly hadn't thought he would be this close this soon." She took another deep breath and the cold sweat began to disappear. Her heart slid back down into her chest and resumed its comforting beats. "We can do this," she smiled at Linx. "After sleep though. I think we both need to rest for the night. I may be wide awake right now but that's not going to last for long." She rubbed both of her hands over her face and sighed. "Ok, closest hotel. Let's go." She smacked her hands on her knees and chuckled.

Linx gave a tired smile in return and shifted the car in gear. His body was slowly going back to normal. His heart wanted nothing more than to unwind. They moved back out onto the road and looked for signs of a place to stop. Unfortunately, it was very dark and mostly deserted. But they kept their eyes open and hoped for something to pop up, both of them slowly losing their adrenaline rush and slipping back to their exhausted states.

•   •   •   •   •

Haydeez awoke with a start. She bolted up in her bed, face covered in sweat, heart racing. "Linx! I have an idea!" she yelled. She scrambled out of bed and caught her foot on the sheet. With a grunt, she hit the floor. "Damn it!" As she pulled herself up, she shoved Linx and said, "Get up. I have an idea and it's really good. You have to hear it. Come on." She sat on his bed and bounced up and down. "Come on, come on, come on," she exclaimed over and over.

Linx flipped over, pulled the sheet out from under her, and knocked her back on the floor with a tiny yelp. "Hey!" she yelled.

He laughed and leaned over the side of the bed. "I didn't know you were there."

She shoved his face and said, "Come on, punk!" She jumped up and ran to the bathroom to get dressed.

As Linx watched her run away, his heart fluttered. He loved seeing her like this, full of enthusiasm, like a child at Christmas. A part of him hoped that one day she would look at him with the same emotion. The other parts told him to shut up and quit whining. He slid out of bed and grabbed his pile of clothes to get dressed. He pulled off his superhero pajama pants as the bathroom door clicked open. "You must really want to go. I don't even have my pants on yet." He looked at Haydeez, dumbfounded.

She scoffed. "Do I have to dress you myself to get it done?"

Linx paused with his jeans in his hand and thought. "No, I'm gonna let that one go." He bent to put them on. His movements were intentionally slow to irritate her. As he snuck a glance, he realized he probably should have moved faster. Haydeez stood on the other bed and swung a pillow at his head. There was a grunt followed by, "Ok, I'm moving!" and within minutes they were out the door.

Once they got to the car, Haydeez started to explain her plan.

"Are you crazy? It's bad enough we'll have to eventually fight him, but you want to do it twice? What's wrong with you?" Linx asked, completely against her idea. His stomach did flips just thinking about it.

"Ok look, we don't actually have to confront him directly. But we know he's got the stag and we need it. What if we get one of the pack to do it for us? We could pull one of the people in the back, talk to them, convince them that we're right, and then get them to steal it from him. It could work," she said eagerly. "We're so close. We have to at least try something." She pulled out the tracker and showed it to Linx. "Look, the dots are getting closer together and further away from us. We can't let him win. I'm going to do this whether you want to or not. I'd just prefer to have some back up if I needed it." A pleading smile spread across her lips and she tilted her head to the side. "You know you want to. Come on, it'll be fun."

Linx scoffed. "Not really my idea of fun but alright, I'll do it." He grudgingly agreed.

Haydeez clapped her hands and bounced up and down. "Yay! Now let's go find them and take the stag so we can wake up Cernunnous and he can kill his Alpha." She paused and thought about what she said. "Ok, I see where you'd be nervous about this. It doesn't really hit you till you say it out loud." She laughed. "Oh well, time to go steal a wooden stag."

Linx rolled his eyes and chuckled. "Right, if we can even get that close. Let's hope the rest of the pack doesn't like the new management." He shook his head and shifted the car into gear. "Where to, love?"

Haydeez pointed northeast and they headed out onto the nearly empty highway in the early morning light.

•   •   •   •   •

It did not take long to find the pack. No matter how hard the Alpha pushed them, they still needed rest. Haydeez and Linx followed the blinking dot until they were practically on top of the pack.

The Alpha had managed to find a spot where they were covered and protected from eyes. There were a couple of men that walked around the pile of dogs and humans while they slept. The two men yawned and continued their watch. Large bags hung under their bloodshot eyes. They moved very slowly, like there was only so much energy left and they expended all of it by just breathing.

Haydeez crouched down behind a bush and barely whispered to Linx, "Two awake. We only need one. Don't move." She turned back to the pack and pulled something shiny out of her pocket. She caught the sun and flashed a couple times at one of the men.

He turned quickly to see the source. He took a few steps towards her hiding place and squinted. When she caught the sun again, the man's eyes grew wide. He glanced nervously at the sleeping pack and the Alpha curled up at the other end. The man quickly made his way to the bush and leaned around it to see what was there. When he found nothing, he paused. He just assumed he had gone crazy from lack of sleep. Then there was another flash behind some trees a little further away. So, he followed it.

After a few minutes of the chase, Haydeez stepped out from behind a tree and whispered, "Please don't yell. I don't want to hurt you. I need to talk to you." She held up her hands to show one empty and one with a mirror. "Can we talk for a minute?" she asked cautiously.

The man looked back to where the pack was and shuddered. His hands shook and his forehead had little beads of sweat in spite of the chill in the air. His eyes were wide with fear. He did not act like a pack warrior, but like a scared child.

He took a shaky breath. "Who are you?" he asked with one eye on Haydeez and one eye on the direction he had come from.

"A friend." She paused and took in every movement the man made. His posture and actions told her more than he could ever say as his eyes flicked back and forth and his muscles twitched beneath the skin. She could tell she had to be careful with him to ensure his own fear did not overpower his desire to be away from the Alpha. She tested the waters. "You're scared of him. That's very obvious. If you hear me out, I'll tell you how I can help you." Haydeez remained still. She did not want to spook the man. He was already jumpy enough.

"How do I know I can trust you? I don't even know you," he asked nervously. He wiped his palms on his pants.

"Look, the Alpha isn't a good person. I don't know what happened but I know he's killed a lot of people since he came back. Am I right?" she asked. The man nodded quickly. "He thinks you're weak doesn't he?" He nodded again. "If you help me, I'll make sure that he never hurts your pack again."

"He hates women," the man blurted. "He'll kill you before you get close enough to do anything."

Haydeez smiled calmly. She tried to remain as far from intimidating as possible. "I believe you. But you have to trust me. I'm not just an ordinary woman. I can handle myself but I need you to do something for me. Do you think you can do something to help me?"

He looked back the way he came and just stared for a long time. His heart raced and he was covered in sweat at that point. His hands shook feverishly. Finally, he turned around and said, "Yea, I can do something for you if you promise that he'll never hurt us again. You have to give me your word. If I'm going to endanger my pack, I need to know it's worth it." He licked his lips and wiped the sweat from his face.

Haydeez reached a hand out to the man. "I give you my word. If you help me, I *will* stop him." She held his eyes.

His shoulders relaxed and he exhaled audibly. He took her hand in his and shook vigorously. "What do you need me to do?"

· · · · ·

It did not take long to explain what she needed. A few minutes later, the man made his way around the mass of dog and human. The pack had pretty much fallen asleep where they stopped. There were dogs sprawled on top of humans and vice versa. He stepped lightly to avoid waking anyone. He could feel his blood as it pounded in his head. The realization of what he was about to do snuck up in the back of his mind, threatened to paralyze him.

Haydeez watched from the bushes, downwind. She had sent Linx back to the car, just in case things did not go as planned. She wanted to know that Linx would have the car ready. Her breath was still as she watched, her eyes on the man but still hidden.

He tripped over a paw and froze. She could see how wide his eyes were even from her hiding place. Inside she calmly told him to keep going.

He looked down at the animal as it slept and let out a sigh. The Alpha had pushed the pack so hard that they just collapsed and took complete advantage when they had the chance. The dog remained asleep, tongue out, totally oblivious to anything around it. If the rise and fall of the chest was not visible, it would look dead. He took a step and slowly moved further around the pile.

The man could feel a headache coming on with each step. The fear was starting to take over. He was not part of the original pack. He was an outsider to the Alpha. However, being born into the pack was still valuable. He would probably not see grey hair for many decades to come and his metabolism kept those fat pockets away that other middle aged men had. He learned how to hunt like a predator and not be afraid of injury because scrapes and bruises would heal within minutes and the more serious wounds would heal within a few hours or a day at the most.

For him, being pack meant family, safety and freedom. He knew the moment Gavin came into their lives, all those things would be taken away. The human women and children had already been killed. His heart ached at the thought of what they had done to all those innocent people. At one point he had chosen to take a human mate. They did not have any children yet but he had loved her. He would remember her face, her eyes full of terror when she was ripped apart. He could sometimes taste her blood still. Nothing could ever make him forgive himself for what he had done, what he had been forced to do to her. All he could do was hope that when he helped this stranger, it would atone for everything and he could die in peace one day. He hoped to be reunited with his mate in death.

After several heart stopping moments, he reached the Alpha. He was in the Loup Garou form and was asleep apart from the pack. He did not want them to touch him with their human bodies. So he picked a spot in the sun, his body sprawled out on his back. Andrew took a tentative step and tried to stay downwind for as long as possible.

From the moment they arrived in the British Isles, Gavin had spent more and more time as the Alpha and less time as the human. Most of the pack believed that his mind was lost to the creature at this point. They had no idea how right they were.

The man watched the Alpha breathe. He was close enough to see warm little puffs of air escape his snout. The fur on his muzzle rustled with each exhale. The creature remained still except for the silent rise and fall of his massive chest. He could see the stag displayed in the brown fur of the beast's chest.

Everything froze for a moment. Haydeez strained her eyes as she tried to see what happened but she was too far away to see clearly.

The man stood over the Alpha, terrified. He licked his lips a few times and wiped sweat from his forehead. He rubbed his hands on his pants trying to gain the strength to do what needed to be done. His heart was beating so fast it sounded like the purr of an engine. His hands shook as he watched, unsure if he was doing the right thing.

After several moments mustering the courage to move, he finally took that last step. With his heart in his throat, he silently inhaled and held his breath. Sweat beads collected on his forehead as he crouched down slightly and moved his right hand towards the stag. Haydeez held her breath as well, as if breathing would disturb the scene.

Had he thought it through, the man might have turned down her offer. Maybe he should have. His fingertips brushed the wood and he thought he had succeeded. It was at that moment that the Alpha inhaled deeply, breathed in all the scents close to him. What the man had forgotten was that, moments ago, he had taken Haydeez by the hand to seal their agreement. To a normal person, the gesture would not have mattered. To the Alpha, with all of his senses spiked, his hand reeked of a female.

The creature's eyes flew open and locked on the man. In a movement that seemed too quick to actually happen, the Alpha had him by the throat and stood up with the smaller man in his hand. He lifted the man and growled. "You dare come to your Alpha stinking of some female," he snarled. Saliva dripped from the corner of his mouth. His ears twitched as he sniffed the air. "You smell of fear but not sex. Why would you have a female's scent on you if you didn't mate with her?" he asked, head cocked to the side.

Haydeez had to stop herself before she yelled out.

It was obvious that the man who used to be inside was now lost. The creature's instinct was to hunt, kill, and mate. To him, if a female did not serve one of those three purposes, they were useless. He did not understand. He sniffed the air again. Perhaps he had missed the subtle scent.

The man glanced down for a split second and then squeezed his eyes shut. A wave of fear and pain cascaded off of his body and flowed down the creature's arm into his face. He wiggled a little to loosen the creature's grip on his throat. He started to feel light headed as the blood was cut off from his brain. His fingertips began to go numb.

The Alpha looked down to where the man had looked and a light came on inside his head. "You'd steal from your Alpha?" he growled. "I promise you an eternal life taking what you want, giving nothing in return and this is what I receive as thanks?" His grip tightened. "You try to steal from me?" he yelled, spittle flew at the man's face. "Where is she, mutt? She's close by. She'd have to be. Where's she hiding?" The tip of his claws poked through Andrew's skin on his neck; blood trickled slowly down.

Haydeez crouched lower behind the bush and did not make a sound. If she could avoid the Alpha for now she would. She tried to make herself as small as possible.

The Alpha looked around, smelling the air to see if he could catch her scent. "It appears that you've chosen your side, mutt. You want to side with some dirty female, then she can join you in hell when I find her." He lifted the man higher and squeezed his throat a little tighter causing more blood to flow.

That was enough to make Haydeez move. "Hey!" she shouted as she jumped up. "If you've got a problem, deal with me. I'm the dirty female," she said as she took a step around the bush.

A wicked grin spread across his half canine face as he said, "Breakfast. And who will I be dining on this morning?" His tongue flicked out and caressed an elongated canine. The saliva spread across the shiny white surface.

"The only thing you'll be eating is grass when I pound your face into the ground. Put him down and maybe I'll go easy on you, but I'm not making any promises," she said, her hands moved behind her back. She grabbed the silver daggers she had strapped to her back under her shirt and just stood there waiting for him to make his move. Inside her head, she silently hoped he would stay right where he was. She knew she was not ready for this but she was not about to hide while the Alpha tore apart the man that tried to help her.

A growl escaped the Alpha's throat. It rumbled across the pack and woke anyone who was still asleep. They all turned, like a wave of faces, to focus on the stranger at the end of the field. "You want me to release him?" The creature dug his claws into the meat of the man's throat and shook him violently. Blood sprayed everywhere as the limp body was tossed around. Then the Alpha threw him to the ground and yelled, "You do *not* give me orders! I'm the Alpha and you're nothing!"

"No!" Haydeez yelled in a feeble attempt to protect the man that tried to help her. Everything inside her felt cold. She watched as his body twitched and landed on the grass and the last bits of his life flowed out of him in a dark puddle. A weak smile spread across his lips as he closed his eyes for the last time. She shivered as everything hit her all at once. This creature planned to kill her without another thought. He desperately wanted her dead and all she could do was think of how she just let that poor man down. A lump formed in her throat. Her gaze turned back to the Alpha who looked her dead in the eyes. An eerie feeling of despair flooded over her.

Anger began to prickle over his body and came off of him in hot waves that flowed over his pack and forced the change for those that were still human.

Haydeez watched as the humans reshaped into large dogs like the others, their clothes sunk into their skin to be replaced by fluffy fur coats. If the sight was not disturbing enough, they all began to drop their front paws to the ground and faced the Alpha.

He had forced them to prostrate themselves before him but never took his eyes from Haydeez. The little show was more to display his power and the respect that he demands and less about any feeling he got from the action itself. He challenged her, taunted her with his stare. He wanted to scare her, to taste her fear, and spit it back in her face in disgust. He waited for her to make a move, put up a fight, or be a worthy opponent. He leaned back his head and let out a howl that rippled across the field. The pack chimed in and the chorus began.

If she was not on the receiving end of this hunt, she would have thought the sight was beautiful. It was enough to bring about that primal emotion in every predator. But the moment he took his eyes from her and leaned back his head, her body was in motion. She was not stupid. She knew she would have to take down each and every pack member in order to win. One hundred to one was really not the best odds for her. So she ran. Her legs moved faster than her brain. Her mind almost did not see the fallen tree in time. Her heart skipped a beat as she saw it at the last second and hopped over it. She raced around trees and over hills until she could see the car with Linx in the driver's seat.

Behind her she could hear the sounds of the hunt. The Alpha led the pack and she was the unfortunate prey. Beneath her feet, she could feel the vibrations of every canine that had just scented her. In her wake was the sound of hundreds of paws as they hit the dirt and kept time with the pulse of the earth itself. Her legs pumped faster. "Start the car!" she shouted frantically. "Now!" She waved her arms at Linx.

The car purred to life and he leaned over to open her door. Haydeez jumped inside and yelled, "Go!" Dirt and grass kicked up behind the tires as they peeled out of the clearing and headed back towards the road.

The Alpha burst from the trees and landed heavy in the clearing, his pack on his heels. They pounded the ground as they raced after the car. White puffs flew from their muzzles and spittle fell from their teeth. Their prey looked like it could escape and they would not allow it because the Alpha controlled their desires. They felt every emotion the Alpha felt and the only thing in his mind was kill.

Linx swerved. His eyes darted between the almost non-existent path and the sharp teeth coming up quickly behind him. He did not realize he held his breath but he also did not have time to remember to breathe. His knuckles turned white on the steering wheel. The engine roared with every turn. They could see the road ahead.

The car lurched to the right. Haydeez whipped her head around. She could feel her skin turn cold. Butterflies danced in her stomach as she looked behind them. Up close, the Alpha looked even more terrifying and determined. He slammed his body against the side of the car, rage emanated from his eyes. Even beneath the fur, she could see his muscles flex and tense. It was not that she was afraid of the Alpha. It was the fact that they passed fifty on the speedometer and he kept pace comfortably.

"You better make this little car go faster, Linx. Looks like we're not going to lose him anytime soon," she said in an attempt to remain as calm as possible. Her voice had a slight tremble. "At least the pups can't keep up," she laughed. Her attempt at levity was lost on Linx.

He glanced at Haydeez and then back to the trees. "You're not funny you know. I'm trying to avoid trees and teeth here," he said, as he finally remembered to breathe again. His breath and pulse acted like he ran the whole time.

"And claws," Haydeez pointed out.

"Not helping."

"Sorry, gun's in the trunk."

"Damn it!" He yelled as he pressed harder on the gas. He could see the road ahead and hoped nobody was coming. The car swerved around a tree and barely missed a branch. It scraped across the roof. Linx laughed. "Ha! I remembered it this time!"

Haydeez watched as the Alpha slowly fell behind. "I think we may have found his top speed. Lucky us," she said sarcastically as she let out a breath. Her heart refused to slow down.

"Hold on please," Linx said as he jerked the wheel to the right. Tires squealed on the pavement. Haydeez had one hand on the grip above the door and the other on the armrest in the middle of the seats. The smell of burnt rubber filled the morning air. Smoke puffed up from the tires. The little car protested but Linx insisted and they squealed onto the highway headed north. They tried to stay just enough ahead of the Alpha to avoid getting eaten.

"That's right! You stay back there!" Linx yelled. "I win!" He exhaled loudly and glanced at Haydeez.

Both hands still braced her body as she looked back at Linx and laughed.

The creature slid to a halt before it reached the road. The smell of rubber and gasoline assaulted his nostrils and he snorted angrily. A growl rumbled in his belly and bubbled up into his chest as he watched the vehicle speed off down the road. "I *will* taste your blood soon enough, female. This isn't over yet. You still need me," he snarled, an inhuman grin spread across his canine jaws.

He sat back and placed his front paws on the ground. He leaned his body forward and released a deep, promising howl. It called out to his pack, urged them to make haste. It warned his prey that they would soon meet their demise. His cry released all the anger and disgust for the human race, let anyone nearby know that this battle may have been lost but the war was not over until he tasted that familiar warm, metallic liquid as it gushed from her open throat and flowed down his.

Chapter 27

Snowflakes dusted the ground in a small town on the southern tip of the Isle of Arran. The wind picked up as a storm was rumbling off in the distance. White-capped waves rushed the shore.

A short man with dark hair stood in front of the entrance to a dock. He pulled his hat down tight as the wind threatened to steal it from his head. His thick wool jacket kept the elements from reaching his skin. The words he heard, however, lead the chilled evening air straight to his bones. He shook his head vigorously and said, "There's no way I can take ye out there in this. We'll capsize fer sure."

Haydeez had to speak up to be heard over the sound of the storm rushing in to meet them. "But we have to get out to that island now. I'll pay you anything." She pulled her windbreaker up around her neck, her hair whipped around her head.

"What could ye possibly need on that island? Tis just a lighthouse and nobody's home anymore," he said. He had to hold onto a post as a particularly strong gust charged over the dock. "It's not smart to be settin sail in this, lass. Yer askin for trouble. You an' yer boyfriend will have to come back tomorrow." He tried to push them away but they refused to move.

"Look, you have no idea what'll happen if we don't get out there now. I don't care if I have to take a boat and ferry myself out there. Hell, it's not that far. Maybe I'll just swim. But no matter what, I need to be on that island now. Either you can take me and ensure that I get there safe or I can try to swim it and die. Which do you think would be the more appropriate option?" Haydeez yelled above the rushing sounds.

Linx swung his arm out and tried to grab hold of anything as his feet slipped out from under him. Haydeez reached out and grabbed him before he fell to the ground. "Thanks, love. Are you sure we need to do this now? Maybe he's right. Maybe we should wait." A mixture of rain and snow began to fall all around them. "Right. This is just bloody fantastic!" he yelled.

She turned to Linx and moved close to him. She tried to talk low so the old man could not hear. "We have to put the pieces in place before the Alpha gets here. If we don't, we're screwed. The storm will slow him down and by the time he gets here we'll be ready for him. It'll give us the chance to prepare ourselves. We have no other choice, Linx. It has to be now." She gripped his shoulder tight and stared into his eyes. Her gaze urged him to move forward.

The old man cleared his throat. "Ye best be gettin a room and come back in the morning. I can take ye then." He tried to shove them again. "Go on now, move along."

Haydeez glanced at Linx who nodded in understanding. Linx grabbed the old man with his one good arm and dragged him off the dock. In a blur of feet and fists, the man fought and yelled. Linx had his arms, one in a cast still, under the old man's arms and locked them behind the man's head to prevent him from getting in any good swings. It was an awkward hold considering Linx was still injured but he brushed off the pain and did his part to keep the old man busy while Haydeez made her way to the boat.

Haydeez raced down the dock and hopped in a row boat that was barely tied down. She dropped her bag on the wet floor of the boat and looked back at Linx. "Let's go! Move it!" she yelled.

Linx dropped the old man on the ground and said, "I'm totally going to hell for this." He ran down the dock as he yelled over his shoulder, "Sorry! Promise we'll bring it back!" He quickly untied the single rope that kept the boat from floating out to sea and hopped in. He grabbed a paddle and started to row out to the tiny island with the lonely lighthouse.

The old man jumped up and yelled, "I warned ye! If ye die, it's no blood on me hands!" He shook his fist once before he turned around and headed for the little house about a hundred yards away. He mumbled to himself the whole time about all these damn kids and their crazy ideas.

The current was strong and pushed against the tiny row boat. Under better conditions they probably could have swam out to the island. The lighthouse kept them on track as the sky grew darker and the air became colder. Haydeez had her hood flipped up and the drawstring pulled tight. Linx wiped his face in a futile attempt to see where they were headed. The medication had begun to wear off and his arm throbbed but he knew that Haydeez could not do it on her own, regardless of those tattoos her dad gave her when she was younger. So, he pushed himself and fought through the pain.

It took longer than they thought but Haydeez and Linx made it safely to the island. Haydeez jumped out and dragged the boat onto the shore so it would not get pulled into the sea. She reached over to help Linx stand when something occurred to her. She cocked her head to the side and paused. Her mind was so focused that she did not hear Linx yell at her. At that moment, she realized that they were indeed in the right spot. They had found Cernunnous's prison.

She looked down at her feet. All around her the ground was lush and green. Flowers were in bloom, full of vibrant colors. Birds sang a chorus of beautiful songs behind her. She thought she even heard a few crickets. A triumphant smile spread across her lips. "Do you hear that?" she asked in her normal voice. There was no reason to yell anymore. The sound of the wind and the crash of the waves had disappeared. She untied her hood and pushed it back. The sunset illuminated her golden hair and made her face glow. Her whole body was warm like nature had skipped fall and winter and jumped right back into spring.

Linx was yelling. "Haydeez, what the bloody hell is wrong with you?" He tripped getting out of the boat and almost landed on his face. He shivered and got back up. He shook her shoulders and asked, "Have you gone mad? All I hear is this storm. What's wrong with you?" He watched her look around with an expression of pure happiness. He grabbed her face and turned it so her eyes were focused on him. "Haydeez!"

"Linx, it's so beautiful. Don't you see it? I've never seen anything like it."

"See what? There's nothing but dirt and rocks here. I think we're in the wrong place."

"The island, it's amazing, so bright. Can't you see it?"

"Haydeez, you've gone mad. It's dark and cold and wet here. Let's get to the lighthouse until the storm passes. We'll figure out what to do once we're dry." Linx grabbed her by the arm and started to walk towards the light.

"No, we're here. We're in the right place, Linx. This is it. It has to be," she said excitedly. Her eyes sparkled and her heart raced from the exhilaration. "How do you not see all this?" She turned to him, a look of sadness and confusion passed over her eyes. Then it hit her. With her eyes wide, she dug deep into her pockets. "The pieces! I've got all the pieces!" She pulled out one of the keys and handed it to Linx. "Now can you see?" she asked with anticipation.

Linx had to grab onto her shoulder to steady himself. His eyes were wide and his mouth hung open as he tried to take in everything he saw. The sound of the storm disappeared to be replaced by the buzzing of bees and birds singing their happy melodies. "Bloody hell!" He looked at the grass, the flowers, and everything Haydeez had seen just moments ago.

"You can see it! Isn't it amazing?" She took his arm and they walked toward what was a lighthouse moments ago.

Now, what stood before them was a small chapel with a single candle flickering in the tower where a bell would normally hang. Off to one side stood a tall tree with full green leaves and birds nestled in every nook.

"It was a spell. They kept it hidden with a spell. I can't believe they used magic when it's against everything they believe," Haydeez said, still in awe. "We've got to put the pieces in before he gets here. I want to make sure his is the last key that needs to be turned." She rushed toward the large tree as her heart still raced. She looked like a kid at Christmas running to a big pile of presents.

Linx followed her, a renewed feeling of energy and calm reaching deep inside. He felt the warmth as it emanated from the island itself. He stood side by side with Haydeez in front of the tree and just stared. In his hand, the piece happily pulsed and called out to the tree.

Haydeez ran her fingers over the bark like she was searching for something. "There's nothing here, no holes, no grooves, nothing," she said. "How do you put a key in a lock when you can't see the lock?" The daunting task and the overwhelming opposition was beginning to take its toll. Her shoulders slumped and she sighed. "I don't know what to do anymore."

Linx looked at her and burst into an almost uncontrollable fit of laughter. "If you don't know what to do, I guess we're bloody well screwed." He put his hand on the tree to steady himself as he continued to laugh. "Maybe if we hide, the big bad wolf won't find us." He could not help himself. The words just continued to spew out of his mouth without checking with his brain first. "He really doesn't like you, love. He's probably on the other shore right now trying to figure out how to get across."

Haydeez backhanded Linx so hard it threw him to the ground. "What the hell is wrong with you? We're both going to die if I don't think of something and you're laughing. How about you do something useful for a change? Instead of being you, how about you be me for tonight? I'll play the part of the idiot sidekick and you can play the hero for once. You think this is easy?" she yelled.

"If I don't laugh, I'll panic and the last thing we need is for me to flip out." He looked up at her from the lush green grass he was crouched on, blood dripped from the corner of his mouth. "I can't help it," he said as he wiped the blood away. "If I could think of something, I would. I wish I could do more." He stood up and brushed himself off. "What do you want me to do? Apologize for not being more useful to you? Fine. I'm sorry I'm such a lousy waste of your precious time." He put his hand on the tree again.

The island began to shake. It was a small ripple like a tremor but still noticeable. They looked at each other for a moment. At the same time, they both turned to the tree. Where Linx's hand was pressed against the bark, there was an indent in the shape of an eagle in flight. He lifted his hand slowly and turned it over. On his palm was a red smear from where he had wiped the blood off his lip. He looked up at Haydeez. "Ha! I opened the grooves!" A triumphant grin spread across his lips as he began to dance around the tree.

Haydeez just stood there and stared at the tree. "A blood sacrifice. I should've known." She pulled a knife from a sheath at her back and sliced her hand open. She winced and looked at the fresh wound she had inflicted. Blood pooled in her palm in a warm, red puddle. She slapped her hand against the bark and held her breath. Her heart skipped a few beats as, one by one, animal shaped grooves opened up on the trunk. She exhaled with a chuckle. "They're open. I need the pieces. Hurry." She reached out and waited for Linx to hand her the one she had given him a few moments ago.

"Then I'll be left in the rain again. I don't know about that," he said. "I quite enjoy the dry land and the little birds and all that." He stopped and stood next to the tree. "Put yours in first." He paused and added, "Wow that sounded horrible." He chuckled.

Haydeez rolled her eyes and reached into a pocket. "Fine, big baby." Without a thought, she held her breath and put the first piece into the tree.

•   •   •   •   •

It was just past dark when a phone rang. There was a pause and then a voice answered. "Yes?"

"They landed on the island. I've done as ye asked. The third man is not here yet. Would you like for me to call when he is?" an old voice asked.

"Of course and I'd like to know the outcome as well. I have confidence that the woman will do her job properly but I'd like confirmation for the sake of the other members. You've done well so far. You'll be pleasantly rewarded if you continue to please the Council," Peter said. "As soon as it's done, remember that."

"Aye, sir. I'll be watching all nigh if I have to," the old man said. "They have me boat."

"I'll be waiting for your call," Peter said and hung up before the old man could respond.

The old man looked at the phone and shook his head. He hung it up and went to his window to look out on the storm that had whipped up out of nowhere and taken over the tiny island with the lonely lighthouse. He could not see Haydeez or Linx because the rain and snow was too thick but he knew they made it.

Magic flowed off the island and trailed over the choppy waters. It snaked its way up the short pier to the lonely house on the opposite shore. As soon as Haydeez had set foot on the beach, a pulse rippled through the line and touched the wizard to tell him that someone had been able to see through his spell. At that moment he knew he could call Peter and tell him that everything was going according to plan.

For many years, his fellow brothers were chosen to station themselves at this post, to watch over the chapel and the tree. It was an honor to be chosen as the guardian of the lighthouse. He was proud that all their work had taken them to this point and he was the one to see the end. His eyes searched through the dark in an anxious attempt to make out a figure, a movement, or anything. He wanted desperately to be there for the final moments but he knew he would have to be the one to report back to the Council and that was more important than anything he wanted to do.

So, he sat and watched through the rain and snow for any sign that the life's work of many generations of guardians was finally coming to a close. He sighed, "Soon, the end will come. I warned him the lass may not come out of this. Her blood won't be on my hands," he mumbled to himself, a deep foreboding caused his accent to sound eerie and slightly demented.

Chapter 28

The sound of paws smacking the mud echoed over the hills in southern Scotland. Every member of the pack ran in dog form. They were too close now to have anyone fall behind. The Alpha insisted the canines move faster. He forced each member into their alternate form and drove them hard.

After his encounter with Haydeez, he wanted nothing more than to tear her apart and feast on her insides. His anger and desire were so intense that his emotion flowed off his fur and clouded the minds of his pack as well. He overwhelmed them with his own want and need to kill her. It was the fuel that compelled them to continue without rest. Not even the icy rain or the wind as it howled in their ears could deter them. It was almost as if the storm was the precursor to the pack's arrival.

A bolt of lightning chased an unseen foe across the sky. Thunder followed immediately. The clouds swirled and collided in an eerie dance in the darkness. The air was alive with electricity. Lightning illuminated the Alpha's eyes, so full of rage and bloodlust. Even as the rain matted down the rest of his fur, his hackles rose, making an intimidating figure even more threatening. It was intoxicating. He passed it on to his pack. One by one, they contracted the fever and fell victim to its destruction. Their blood pumped pure adrenaline. They panted with exhaustion, stomachs growled with hunger, but they pressed on as one unit. The only desire they felt was death. Haydeez needed to die. Cernunnous needed to die. Anyone who stood in their way would die. Blood would flood the waters around the island tonight.

Chaos had been called. The dogs of war were unleashed. Nobody was safe tonight.

• • • • •

"The last one's here. He's got a pack of dogs with him. What should I do?" the old man asked, eyes focused on the horde as it approached his pier.

"Leave them be. They're supposed to reach the island. Just stay where you are and call me when it's over. The hour is no concern. I require confirmation of the completion of the task," Peter said.

"Aye, I'll be calling you soon enough." He paused. "They be taking to the water now. The big one has them swimming out to the island now. Shouldn't be much longer," he squinted to see them through the waterfall on his window.

"Very good. Your brothers would be proud of your work."

The old man puffed up at the complement. All he wanted was the recognition he deserved for everything he did to keep this secret hidden. "Thank you," he said right before the phone clicked. He held the phone and his breath for a moment as he caught sight of the pack again. The waves seemed to swallow them up and then spit them out above the crest. He pulled himself away long enough to hang up the phone and then turned back to watch the wave of dogs become one with the churning waters.

• • • • •

The Alpha growled at the sting of the icy waters as they touched the skin of his exposed belly. He could feel the shock as it hit each and every one of his pack. With every stroke, he forced his heat out to the pack to ensure they moved forward. The heat of his emotion, raw and pure, warmed their bodies and pressed them into the cold.

As hard as it was for the boat to make it to the island, it was monumentally more difficult for the entire pack to swim from the pier to the beach. The pack mentality was the only thing that kept them going. The Alpha pumped their adrenaline with thoughts of hunting their prey. He reached out to each of them with his warmth and hatred. His soul caressed their primal instincts. He used everything he ever learned about stalking and savoring the kill and pushed it out to touch that spot deep in the core of every dog, that place that longs for the taste of hot, fresh blood. He touched every sense, every nerve to ensure they were ready. By the time the last dog reached the water, none of the pack could feel the sting anymore. They were numb to every sense. They only felt the hunger.

His paws touched ground under the waves. He dug in with his claws and pulled his body up to the muddy beach. Slowly each dog emerged from the water, soaked and hungry for blood. A surge of excitement flooded their senses as they looked around the island.

The Alpha stood tall and proud. Around his neck was the last piece of the puzzle. He had to pause at the shock of what he now saw all over the island and what was no longer there. The sun had set hours ago but the moon was full and clear. Tonight it hung high above, a red hue masked its normal glow. The Alpha stretched his neck and rolled his shoulders as he looked up to the night sky. He released a howl that reverberated and rippled over the backs of the dogs. The howl continued as the chorus on the beach picked it up. Through him, the others could see everything. His sight was their sight. The pack stepped into the peaceful scene. They shivered with excitement as the intensity from the island mixed with the Alpha's emotions.

Amidst the call, the Alpha stopped and said, "The Hunter's Moon guides me tonight. All the pieces are in place for my victory." He began to walk up the beach towards the little chapel and the tree that quietly stood it's vigil beside it.

•　　　•　　　•　　　•　　　•

Linx hid in the chapel, silent and anxious. He held the one thing he had brought to protect himself, a silver knife etched with archaic symbols. He would probably die in the process but he hoped the symbols would be enough to take some of the pack with him.

Haydeez paced by the window that faced the beach. She stopped every now and then to see if anyone had arrived. Outside of the island it was dark, the storm still raged, but no sound passed through the invisible barrier the spell had created. She was left completely alone with her thoughts. Everything played out in her head. The Alpha would show up. They would fight for a little while. She might get lucky and steal the last piece. Cernunnous would be released and Haydeez would win. In her head, it worked. She knew that the real world was never as easy as that.

Linx broke the silence. "So you just want me to stay in here and hide?" he said as he looked down at his weapon. "I know I can't do much to help but hiding out here seems like even less than nothing."

She kept her eyes on the window. "I want you to stay here. If something happens to me, at least you can get away once they've left the island. You're not completely healed and all that rowing didn't exactly speed up the process." She glanced over at Linx. "I can't break in a new sidekick this late in the game, remember?" she chuckled.

Linx gave a half-hearted laugh and shrugged. "Yea, I remember." He looked up at her with more emotion than he had expected and added, "To solve all our problems, how about you don't let anything happen to yourself, defeat the crazy immortal wolf thing, and we'll leave the island together. Right? Deal?"

Haydeez relaxed, her body settled into a place of serenity. She smiled with a sigh and said, "Deal, as long as you wait for me here. No matter what."

"You know I'm older than you, love. Technically, I'm only listening because you're a girl," he managed a real laugh.

"And because I could beat you to the ground, tie you up, and make you stay here," she joked.

"Again with the empty promises."

She raised her hand to quiet him, a look of concentration in her eyes. "Shh, do you hear that?" She turned to the window. Outside, still a good distance away, was exactly what she had waited for, but to see it did not make her any more ready to deal with it. The Alpha stood with his pack at his back and sounded the call to begin the hunt. With a slight shudder, she lowered her voice. "Wait here and stay down. Remember, we're leaving together." She smiled.

Linx nodded and watched her walk away from him for possibly the last time. He felt like a rock had been dropped into his stomach. This was wrong but he could not do anything about it. He quietly crawled to the window and positioned himself so he could see everything that happened outside.

He could see the Alpha coming up the path to the chapel and the tree. Goosebumps covered his skin. His heart skipped a beat. This was it - and all he could do was watch.

Chapter 29

The storm had calmed on the island. Outside the spell, the wind still howled, the snow and rain continued to fall in odd directions. Waves crashed against an invisible shore and rushed back out to sea to try again. Inside the protection of the spell, the Alpha could smell the sweet scent of dozens of different flowers. The odor assaulted his nostrils but he brushed it aside in search of a specific smell: the woman. He looked at the tree, then the chapel, and began to make his way up the path, his head held high and a smirk across his canine mouth.

The bloodlust had completely taken over his pack. They marched behind him with only his what he wanted them to feel. Not a single dog scented the ground, barked at the birds, or even stopped to scratch an itch. They should have collapsed on the spot after how hard he had pushed them but they moved like an invisible force was within their muscles, like their minds were no longer their own. An eerie red tint filled their eyes.

The Alpha was about one hundred yards away when he paused. A low growl rumbled up and escaped his mouth. His upper lip curled back in a snarl. Something did not feel right. He looked back at his pack. They looked the way they should but something was off. He looked back at the tree, eyes narrowed, ears twitched. A feeling of claustrophobia began to creep over his mind as his breath increased and his pulse raced. He tried to brush it off but it would not leave.

"You seem a little confused, big guy. Something wrong?" Haydeez stepped around the back of the chapel into view, shotgun slung across her shoulders, silver blade on her hip. "Not having second thoughts are you?" she smirked.

The Alpha shook his head in an attempt to clear his mind. "What did you do to me?" he growled as he tried to make sense of the feeling that washed over him.

"Me? Why would I do something to you? You've been such a pleasure since we met. Wait, could it be that you tried to force my car straight into a tree? Or maybe that you came here with the intent of killing me?" she laughed as she took a couple steps. "But seriously, I didn't do a thing to you. That's not me. It's him." She nodded at the tree. "Maybe you should take a look behind you." She stood between the tree and the chapel and waited.

Aggravated with this feeling that something was not right, he turned around. He looked at his pack and the lush vegetation on the island. "What am I supposed to see, female? The army that I've brought to devour you?" He turned back around to glare at Haydeez. His tail twitched at the tip like it anticipated an attack.

"Look closer," she chuckled. She made a motion with her finger for him to turn around again. "They're not yours anymore, big guy," she whispered.

Enraged, he spun around. Each member of the pack had been full of the bloodlust, so much so that they lost all thought and followed only what he fed them. They swam across a churning canal in the middle of a storm because he wanted them to do it. He had their hearts and their souls. Nobody could break that bond.

What he looked at now was the same pack of dogs but calm. They leaned against each other, slumped on the ground from exhaustion, too tired to even look up when he spoke. It was like the leash had been snapped, and free will had been returned to each of them. Some of them had enough strength left to look in his direction before they closed their eyes for a much needed, and even more deserved rest.

"Get up mutts! Your Alpha commands it!" he yelled. An angry heat began to flow off his body and bubble out around him. "Now!" he growled. The heat flowed over the dogs and drifted off down the path like a warm breeze in the summer. Some of the weaker pack members twitched slightly as their bodies tried to answer the Alpha's call, but they quickly settled back into place and relaxed. The Alpha's blood began to boil. His pack had been taken from him. In a fit of fury, he spun around and snarled at Haydeez.

She flashed him a sweet smile and said, "That wonderful fluttering feeling going through your body is Cernunnous taking back what's his. He's regaining control and man is he pissed at you. He's coming for you, Alpha." She chuckled. "Oh and by the way, he knows why I'm here and he wanted to even the playing field." She motioned behind him. "If someone challenges the Alpha to a one-on-one battle, you have to accept or step aside. Can't have the whole pack doing your dirty work. It's just not fair. You want to be the top dog, you can earn it," she said with a smirk.

He glanced at the tree and subconsciously gripped the stag that hung around his neck. A twinge of fear crept into the back of his mind. "You can't release him without the last piece and I have that," he said. Doubt followed the fear. He was suddenly very unsure of himself. His ears twitched. "You have nothing, female." He spat at the ground.

She glanced down at the ground and said, "Ok, number one, gross. Number two, I have more than you do. When you got here, I'll admit, I was nervous. You're a pretty big guy and I'm just little old me. You had an entire pack of dogs at your command. I have this." She pulled the shot gun off her shoulders and held it out in front. "But now, no pack." She looked him up and down once and added, "And I've fought bigger. Not to mention, without your horde, you're not as scary. So, the way I see it. You have two options. First option, you give me that pretty little piece of wood hanging around your neck and get smacked on the nose by your master. Or," She cocked the gun. "We dance. What's it gonna be, fluffy?"

All around them the energy rose. They could both feel it. It was almost tangible in the air now. Something strong prepared itself and they both knew what it was. Whether he fought or just gave up, the Alpha knew what he had to do. Haydeez could not leave this island if he wanted to survive. She would hunt him till the day she died. He had to kill her and he had to do it now, while Cernunnous was still trapped. Once he dispatched this annoyance he could take care of the Green Man. A low rumble began in his belly.

She chuckled. "So if you're the Alpha does that make me your Omega?" She raised an eyebrow and added, "Tonight I'll be your end." Her lips spread into a wicked smile. "What do you say? The challenge has been extended." She planted her feet and leveled her shot gun. Her hands were steady on the shotgun. She calmed her breathing and he could feel the fear disappear as she retreated into serenity.

The Alpha flexed his hands, muscles pulsed under his fur. "I'll enjoy tasting your blood tonight," he growled. With a movement that looked too swift for a creature his size, he leapt forward at Haydeez, claws first, teeth close behind.

Chapter 30

Linx watched the exchange from his hiding place. His nerves were on end and his stomach did flips. He watched Haydeez casually stroll out into the open and his heart jumped into his mouth. "Please don't let anything happen to her," he breathed.

They talked for a moment but he was too far away to hear what was said. It was very obvious that the Alpha was angry. Linx could feel the heat as it penetrated the tiny chapel and threatened to cut off his air. He took a deep breath and tried to let it out slowly but with each twitch of the creature's muscles, his breath caught in his throat. He could not think straight and it finally clicked in his head. "That's why she wants me in here," he mumbled to himself. At that moment, all he could think about was what he would have to do if she did not make it out of this.

He heard the shotgun cock and froze. Every part of him wanted to burst out of the window and leap in front of Haydeez. His muscles jumped as he sat crouched just out of sight. He never felt so inadequate.

Then he heard it. The shot gun boomed and the Alpha howled. He was not sure if it was pain or anger that caused the sound but the creature continued to move.

• • • • •

Haydeez fired a shot at the Alpha and jumped to the side. She knew the gun would be impractical after the initial shot. With a flick of her wrist, she tossed her useless weapon aside and pulled the knife. The curvy silver blade glittered in the light of the red moon. Her delicate fingers would have looked odd to anyone else wrapped around the handle of something meant to kill, but to her, the specially made weapon fit perfectly in her palm.

The Alpha spun and snorted. Blood matted the fur of his chest around the wounds she had inflicted.

Her heart sank when she saw they had already begun to close. "Ok, so I pissed him off even more. Fantastic," She said as she prepared herself for an attack. She forced her mind to stay where it was and not step back into reality.

With a grunt, the Alpha ran at her again. He swung at her face, claws extended. "I will feel your blood glide down my throat, female," he growled. His paw swiped past her face as she leaned back, just out of reach. A snarl escaped his lips as he turned his paw quickly, swung backwards, and tried to rake his thick claws through her skin.

Haydeez avoided being hit a few times but knew her luck would not last forever. She had to get that last piece in place before he got lucky and took a chunk out of her neck. Her brain focused on how to avoid contact and refused to think about anything else. If she managed to get far enough away for a moment, then she would think of something else. For now, she had to avoid those sharp claws at all costs.

Her eyes fell on the last piece hung around the Alpha's neck and she held her breath. Unfortunately for her, she almost did not see the next attack. The Alpha's paw came up and almost took a chunk out of her stomach. His claw hooked her shirt and ripped a hole to expose the vulnerable flesh beneath. "Hey! I liked this shirt! Damn it."

The Alpha paused. "You care more for your clothing than your safety?" he asked, confusion in his eyes. "I am trying to take your life and yet you remain calm. I have never fought one with such strange convictions," he said. His confusion was short lived. At that moment, he did the only thing he knew how to do: strike. He opened his jaws and leapt at her with more force than an eighteen wheeler. They collided and fell heavily on the ground.

With a grunt, she was knocked to the dirt and trapped under his massive weight. She tried to wiggle out from under him but he had her pinned down tight. In spite of her fall, the knife was still clutched in her hand. With a slight twist, she sank the blade into his flesh. Hot liquid flowed out over her fingers. He jumped up, grabbed his side, and waited for the gash to close. Blood dripped on the ground around his feet.

Haydeez skittered back and held her left arm close to her chest. He had managed to rip open her skin almost down to the bone. Blood stained her shirt and jeans. She hissed as she flexed her fingers. As long as they continued to work, the fight was still on. She pulled herself up with her good hand and bent to pick up her knife. The Alpha still pressed on his side. This was the time she needed. Now she could think.

• • • • •

Linx gasped as the creature knocked Haydeez to the ground. There was a yelp of pain and the creature was off her. Everything happened so quickly it was hard to keep track of the injuries. He silently cheered when he saw the blood drip on the ground all around the Alpha. His excitement was quickly squelched when he saw Haydeez as she cradled her arm. He glanced down at his own injury and thought *bloody brilliant. Now we match.*

He gripped his knife tightly and moved to get up. His heart jumped. The only thing that stopped him was what he saw when Haydeez stood up. There was a look in her eyes that said she had a plan. A wicked grin spread across her lips as she looked up at the Alpha and began to laugh. "We've failed," he whispered.

• • • • •

Haydeez laughed hysterically. The Alpha growled in response. "Your last few moments will be spent this way and you laugh like it's a joke. Is death funny to you, female? Or have you just accepted your fate?" The gash in his stomach closed but not quickly enough. He had to buy some time. He knew he would not die from the wound, no matter how serious but it was still a painful inconvenience.

"A joke? No, I don't think this is a joke. I think you're the joke. You thought this would be so easy, didn't you? You thought I wouldn't be able to put up a fight and that I'd just lie down and die for you," she said as she laughed again and threw her arms up in the air. "You've lost your army, Alpha. Everything you thought you had is gone. The only thing left is that little trinket hanging from your neck. And once I take that, it's over. You're done. That's why I'm laughing. Whether I live or die tonight doesn't matter. All I have to do is survive long enough to take that thing away from you and release that pissed off master of yours. Then he can do whatever he wants with you." She laughed again as she glanced down at her arm. The blood still flowed. "Sure I'll lose a lot of blood, and so what if I die. I guess you were partly right. I've accepted my fate." She shrugged and the laughing stopped, her face stoic. Her pale blue eyes locked tight with his. They trapped him in their icy depths. She tilted her head slightly and leaned forward. In a low voice that almost didn't seem her own, she asked, "Have you accepted yours?"

He did not expect someone so small to have the warrior's spirit that

Haydeez had. He needed something to regain control. He searched for the strength to push forward and fight through the pain and blood loss. The island was full of some kind of energy but he could not grab it. Everything he touched felt cold and foreign to him. His mind hunted frantically for anything to cling to in his time of need.

And then he felt it.

At the edges of his mind, there was a small heat. It flickered and waved at him, taunted him. With all the strength he had left, he reached out for it and held on like his existence depended on it. His body felt warmer the moment he touched it. He looked at Haydeez; his heart raced and his blood burned. "I haven't lost yet, female. You've underestimated the power of an Alpha."

He breathed in deeply and began to quickly heal himself. Blood matted the fur on his stomach but the wound was completely gone. It was like it had not even been there. His eyes burned with a renewed fire as he rolled his shoulders and stretched his neck.

Haydeez could tell something was not right. "Did you just get bigger?" she asked. "Really? Come on!" She threw her hands in the air. "Can't I just fight something that doesn't grow when I'm about to beat it? First the golem, now this?" She looked around and yelled, "I call foul on this one! Unfair!" She grunted and steadied herself. Out of the corner of her eye, she noticed movement in the pack. She did not want to do it but she turned anyway.

Several of the dogs stood up and looked at the Alpha with pleading eyes. They were frozen in place, gaze fixed on their leader. Then, as quickly as they stood up, one by one, their scared eyes rolled back into their heads and their bodies began to drop to the ground. The skin on their faces began to collapse in on the skull. The same thing happened to their ribs and legs. It was like they began to age and lose muscle as fast as she could blink.

She turned back to the Alpha who reveled in his new strength. "You're killing them! You can't do that!" she yelled. Her chest hurt and her stomach threatened to climb up her throat but she pushed it back and stood her ground. "They're innocent. You wanted to take me on but you couldn't even do it on your own. You had to pull their lives away to save yourself. Coward! You're not an Alpha. A real Alpha protects his pack! You've destroyed them! And now it ends." She shifted the knife in her hand so the blade ran along the back of her wrist.

He laughed. Heat emanated off of him. "You still don't understand, female. I should've known you wouldn't get it. Your life means nothing to me. Their lives mean nothing. I can take all the strength I need from these worthless mutts and use it to do what needs to be done!" he yelled. "Once I destroy the Green Man, I'll have all of his power as well, and I can call a whole new generation of pack, dogs that know what it is to follow orders unconditionally. They'll know what it means to respect the leader." He took a step towards her. Before, he had been about two feet taller than her. Now, he stood four feet over her head and outweighed her by several hundred pounds. "This pack will die tonight, along with you and that worthless god trapped in the tree." A deep rolling laugh escaped his canine jaws.

"If you believe that, then take your shot," she said as she planted her feet on the ground. Blood dripped from her lip as she spoke. She could feel every scrape and bruise as her body screamed to stop and give it time to heal. She ignored the pain and ran to that little place in the back of her mind where nobody should ever go. Inside, she found her calm, like the eye of a category five hurricane. The tempest raged all around, lightning flashed and thunder shook the ground, but right there in the middle of it all was nothing but serenity. She planted herself in the center of the stillness and waited.

He charged at her, claws extended and howled. A paw as big as her chest, came straight for her. There was nowhere to go.

So she stood there, prepared to die just to keep him from taking the lives of any more dogs. In a flash, her knife struck out across his knuckles. Blood squirted out and fell to the ground.

His hand burned and he howled but the wound closed up and he came at her again. There was no need to wait to be healed anymore. He had the pack to syphon. She slashed at his wrist but he was too quick. He swung his paw back around and slammed her in the chest. She was tossed across the island. She landed with a grunt as her knife slipped from her fingers. She pulled herself up and scrambled to grab her weapon before he charged again.

"You're through, female. With every breath I take, I grow stronger. Every injury you inflict kills another useless dog. Soon, they'll all be gone and all of this will be for nothing. No matter what you do, I win." He took his time to get to her. She could tell that he knew the eventuality of this scenario. She would run out of strength, but he had an almost endless supply. A wicked laugh rumbled from his jaws as he stood there and watched her make her futile attempt to beat him.

Every muscle in his body bubbled over with heat and power. His blood burned as it rushed through his veins. An eerie glow surrounded him with thin ripples that sparkled as they cascaded down his back that led to different members of the pack. When a shimmering tendril touched someone, they froze and then tumbled to the ground in agony. He pulled from the newest members first, thinned the lines to leave the ones who could fight back until the end.

There was no point to wait anymore. No matter what happened, she would not just sit here and die. A look in her eyes said she was ready for him.

She took off at a run straight at him and yelled. She jumped in the air, knife raised, and slashed at him. Her eyes burned white hot. Every beat her heart took was a laugh in his face as she fought to stay alive for just one more moment.

The Alpha lifted his free hand and tried to push her aside. He barely succeeded but not before she sliced his neck. He was bleeding from two wounds now, the second being only a minor cut.

She kicked at his stomach in a futile effort to slow the healing process. As she hit the ground, she rolled and jumped back up to see him hunched over as more blood bubbled over his claws. Her breath came faster and she smirked at him.

"You will die for this, slow and painful. You've become a flea, biting and scratching for life. But every flea perishes," he growled through gritted teeth.

She glanced at the ground near his feet and saw exactly what she wanted. Right there in a puddle of his blood was the stag. He had not noticed it was gone yet and she took full advantage of that fact.

She ran at him again but this time he turned to face her. He was ready with both of his bloody hands outstretched to grab her. When she was close, she changed position and dropped to the ground. He grabbed her and threw her at the tree. She hit with a thump and a loud gasp. He laughed, "Now, I'll take what's mine."

Haydeez looked back at him, dazed. Her breath came in short gulps as she tried to fill her empty lungs. She shook her head and sucked in a lungful of air. A slow smile spread across her bloodied lips and she chuckled. "Not as tough as I thought you'd be. I'm a little disappointed." She breathed heavy as she tried to prop herself up against the trunk. "I expected so much more."

He crouched down and growled. "I'm tougher than your puny human frame. I've almost completely healed and you still bleed to death. I'd say today was a good day for me." He flexed his hands and tensed his muscles as he watched Haydeez bleed out on the ground. "I think I'll tear open your stomach first and let your insides spill out all around me. You think you can defeat me. Well, I intend to see what you're really made of, female. I want to *taste* what you're made of." He leaned his head back and howled his battle cry. With a look of hunger in his eyes, he charged at Haydeez as she sat helpless and alone under the tree.

Chapter 31

Linx could feel every muscle in his body ache as he watched the scene unfold. His heart dropped when Haydeez hit the tree. He watched as the wind was knocked from her lungs and she tried desperately to breathe again. She was on the ground and blood flowed freely from a large wound, but she never showed fear. She laughed in his face.

Every second that passed was agony. His arm no longer hurt. All he could feel was anger. His only thought was what he planned do to the creature if it took her life.

Then it happened. The beast howled and took off straight for Haydeez.

Linx was torn. Does he keep his promise to Haydeez or does he rush out in a feeble attempt to save her life? In the few seconds that passed, he went back and forth as he chastised himself for one decision or the other. If he had not been right by the window, he probably would not have believed what he saw outside.

As the Alpha raced towards Haydeez, she reached up and slapped the last piece in its designated place with a bloody hand. The moment the piece connected, a wave of heat washed over the island followed by a blinding light. The heat was so intense it stopped the Alpha in his tracks and knocked him back on the ground. He reached up, covered his eyes, and howled in pain.

Members of the pack whined, yelped, and crouched on the ground, eyes closed. The heat pulled them from their sleep and made them pay attention. They huddled together in fear, some shook from the shock of what happened.

Haydeez was knocked face first on the ground next to the tree. She shouldered herself up and squinted to see everything. She saw the Alpha on the ground in a heap about twenty feet away. Out of the corner of her eye, she caught movement in the chapel and waved Linx off so he would stay inside.

A loud crack like a bolt of lightning brought her attention back to the tree. A split had started down the trunk and slowly began to spread. The bark was scorched and smelled like a campfire in the night. As the tree began to fall to the sides, Haydeez dragged herself away to avoid being crushed.

The light faded and the heat lessened. When they could see again, they all looked up at a man still nestled in what was left of the tree. He slowly stretched his arms, pulled himself up, and placed his bare feet on the soft green grass. When he stood at full height, he was well over six feet tall. The helmet of antlers covered in ivy that sat on a bed of long wavy hair the color of untouched charcoal only added to his impressive presence. Animal pelts covered little of his smooth olive skin for the sake of human modesty and nothing else. More strands of ivy sprouted from his hips, trickled down his legs, and held the pelt in place. He moved around, felt all his muscles again for the first time in centuries. In spite of his capture, his body had remained in peak condition. It showed his strength with every bend and twist.

He reached back into the tree and pulled out his staff. Haydeez caught sight of his eyes as he turned back around. They were black as night with twinkling stars fluttering in their mysterious depths. She gasped, completely in awe. Her life had been spent fighting creatures that most people only saw in their dreams. Now here she sat at the feet of a living god. She basked in the warmth of his power, completely dumbfounded.

A booming voice echoed across the tiny island. "I feel your blood. It was you who freed me." He looked down at Haydeez. His words flowed like a babbling brook, slow and casual. "For too long I've been trapped in that cursed tree, cut off from my pack, my followers, their worship. I was slowly dying. To kill a god is not an easy task. To rescue one is an even greater undertaking, one for which I'm eternally grateful." He reached his hand out as leaves grew down his arms. "May I help you up and know the name of my savior?"

Haydeez sat, her body limp, mouth hung open, and her eyes wide. Her heart raced and she could barely hear above the persistent thud in her head. She made a conscious effort to regain her composure and accepted the offered hand. His skin felt baby smooth, too soft to belong to a man who looked the way he did but she was not about to tell him that. The leaves stretched out to touch her skin. "My name," she started to say, her voice crackled slightly. As she cleared her throat, she tried to speak again. "I'm Haydeez," she said. He lifted her effortlessly off the ground.

He cocked his head and looked at her. "Isn't that the name of the Lord of the Greek Underworld?" he asked.

She chuckled and blood bubbled and sputtered out of her mouth. "The spelling's a little different and it's a bit of a story but I was named in his honor. He sort of saved me once." Her cheeks flushed. It sounded funny when she actually heard it. "And you're Cernunnous, right?" She noticed her blood had splattered on his hand and she quickly said, "Oh, that's so disgusting. I'm so sorry." She tried to wipe it away.

The Celtic god nodded. With a smile he said, "It is fine, child. I've gone by many names. That would be the most prominent amongst humans. My pack has other names for me, ones that you wouldn't be able to pronounce." He looked around the island. His eyes fell on the pack in the distance as they quietly dragged themselves to their master. "Come, my children. It's alright," he said softly like a parent talks to a scared toddler.

"No!" the Alpha yelled. "They're mine!" He jumped up to face his master. His fur was matted with dried blood but his wounds had all healed. "They're mine now," he growled.

Cernunnous turned to address the Alpha. "I should've known better than to give you such power. My quest for more power of my own caused me to lapse in judgment." He sighed and shook his head. "Poor Gavin, you've lost yourself. You had such potential. You could've been a great leader on your own but you had so much more to learn."

Haydeez glanced between Cernunnous and the Alpha and said, "I thought gods don't make mistakes."

The Green Man laughed hard. "Of course we make mistakes. Who told you we didn't?"

"Just something I heard along the way," she chuckled.

Cernunnous looked at his pack, ears flat, as they crawled towards him. Their eyes darted between their god and the Alpha. "What have you done to them?" His voice was subdued with a hint of sadness. "What have you done?" he whispered.

"I've tried to turn them into the warriors they should be, not the pathetic mutts you created. They should be ruling this planet. When I found them, they'd gone into hiding. You had an army of indestructible fighters and you turned them into this," he said as he motioned to the scared dogs. "When you left, they ran away with their tails between their legs and hid from humanity. They hid!" he yelled at the dogs.

The god turned to his pack and asked, "Is this true, my children? Did you go into hiding when I disappeared? I'd feared the worst for you but I never thought that would happen. My heart ached for you all these years. When I couldn't feel you, I didn't want to imagine what happened," he said. Sadness filled his eyes.

Kal cautiously stepped forward in dog form and changed into a man at his master's feet. He crouched down, naked and scared. "Master, we didn't know what to do without you. We left our homes and crossed the ocean to the new world. We made homes for ourselves in a place now called Canada. Every day we prayed to you hoping that you'd hear our cries but you never came. As the years went on, our pack grew. Some of us took mates." He motioned back to the females.

Cernunnous raised an eyebrow. "You allowed females into the pack?"

The Alpha smirked and puffed up his chest. He knew how his master felt about females in the pack. "And what happened?"

"We mated. Some of us had children, master. Some of our children could change like us. We didn't have to take over towns anymore. Our pack flourished and we did it without all the killings." He kept his head bowed as he spoke.

The Loup Garou waited happily for Kal to be punished.

"I see. Show me these females and the children. I want to see what you've created," he said calmly.

Kal lifted his head as tears welled in his eyes. A look of pure anguish filled his eyes as he answered. "Master, our mates were killed if they couldn't change. Your Alpha insisted on it. He forced our change and then ordered us to kill any human nearby." He cleared his throat. "But I can show you what's left of our children." He turned to his pack and nodded. Slowly the children of the original pack came forward. They tried to stay as far away from the Alpha as possible. Each one walked up and huddled around their master, their god. "These are all of them?" he asked.

Kal nodded.

"There are more than twenty bodies here."

He nodded again.

"And these are all that's left?"

Kal paused. He swallowed a lump in his throat and nodded one last time.

The Alpha watched smugly in silence. The pack would be punished and he would be seen as the savior. He squared his shoulders and awaited his praise.

Haydeez stood by in silence. She watched everything, unsure what to say. She took off her coat and wrapped it tightly around her arm to protect it. Her head started to feel fuzzy and her body was not as warm as it should be. A wave of nausea rushed over her and she had to steady herself before she collapsed. She sat down on the split tree until the wave passed.

Cernunnous looked thoughtful while everything remained quiet. Even the birds silenced their songs in anticipation of what he would say. The children, male and female alike, cowered at his feet, unsure of the reaction they would receive.

Linx sat at the window, paralyzed. He had seen Haydeez take a seat on the remnants of the tree. He then turned his attention back to the Alpha. He knew if the god wanted to kill her, there was nothing he could do to stop that from happening. But he might have a chance with the Alpha, or so he thought.

After many excruciating moments of silence, Cernunnous spoke. His voice boomed in the silence but managed to maintain a level of calm. "You were the next in line as Alpha. Is that correct, my child?" He looked at Kal as he spoke.

He nodded.

He straightened up and looked down at the children. "You've brought me new pack members tonight. At a glance they look just like the others. It's been too long. I wouldn't have noticed them right away, at least not the males. Why did you tell me about them?" he asked.

Kal looked up and met his master's eyes. "Whether born or chosen, we're all your children. They've worshiped with us and been raised to follow your ways. Yes, we left our home here in Europe but not because we wanted to be apart from you. We left to ensure our safety. When you disappeared, we didn't know if we'd live or die and there were so many who wanted us dead for what we'd done. I made the decision to protect my pack. I couldn't let them be slaughtered because we didn't have your protection anymore. Over the years, we discovered many things about ourselves. One of which was that we could mate and have families and allow our numbers to grow." He glanced at the Alpha out of the corner of his eye and continued. "We'd been told that this wasn't an option. We were misinformed. If I was wrong, then let me be punished. I'll accept whatever you choose to do, but please don't punish them. I'll take all the blame." He stepped forward and dropped his head.

One of the children nudged his hand with her nose and whimpered. The others gathered around his feet and dropped to the ground. They refused to let him step any closer.

Cernunnous watched, a mixture of emotions welled up inside. He chose his pack by the strength of the men in the villages he conquered. Of everything he had been called since the beginning of his time, Master of the Hunt was only one title. "My children, during my time away, I thought about you often. I made you, and then someone took me away from you. No longer could I answer your prayers or guide you. Everything you did was on your own. Every decision you made, every act you took, all of it was yours to do. I see now that my concern wasn't necessary. Here before me stands a man who took my teachings and lived them. He took care of you, nurtured you, allowed you to thrive in the best way." He looked at the Alpha. "You disappoint me, Gavin. You've allowed this part of you to take over." He motioned to the creature that stood before him, the animal that no longer held any part of the man he used to be. "Your lust for blood and power has clouded your every move. The Hunt was only part of our pack. Our entire purpose for being on this planet was to create life. You've taken too many, Gavin, too many unnecessary lives. If my children are unhappy, then I am unhappy." The end of his staff began to glow. "I trusted you to lead my children and instead you've enslaved them."

The Alpha growled. "You've made them weak. I was a true leader. You don't deserve to have the pack anymore. Perhaps once, when we ran together, but now I don't see how you deserve to even live." A wicked grin slid across his jaws and caused an eerie expression that should never be seen on an animal. "Do you know why you were trapped, *Master*?" he growled. "They came to me. They wanted to ensure that their god was the most powerful god in existence. They wanted to trap you, to cut you off from your worthless little followers to ensure that you'd never be able to feel their prayers ever again." He hunched over and flexed his hands, claws extended. "It was me. I gave you to them. I knew that if they trapped you, I could take over the pack and make them what they should've been." His expression turned sour, anger filled his eyes. "They didn't tell me I'd be trapped too. When you were taken, my beast was ripped from me, torn from my body. They separated us, leaving me a mere human. Immortal or not, I was only human." He looked at Haydeez and spit on the ground. "Human like you." He took a step towards her. "Maybe I should punish you for this, *human*."

Haydeez looked up at the Alpha. "Again with the spitting? What is wrong with you?" she asked. Her vision fluttered and there was a rushing noise in her ears. She did not realize how bad the cut was until this moment. She could feel her muscles scream to get up and fight. Her body wanted to move but she just sat there, weak and unsteady, while the Alpha stared daggers through her skull.

"Gavin, your anger is unwarranted. Stand down or I'll force you down," Cernunnous said calmly.

"You can't give me orders anymore. You're no longer my master," he said as he spit on the ground again.

Haydeez was at the point where everything seemed funny, no matter how serious the situation. "He really likes to do that. He's spit at me a few times too." She turned to him and added, "Bad dog. No spitting." She giggled.

The Alpha growled, his muscles twitched, as if he could attack at any moment. He jerked forward like he was charging at her and instantly slammed on the ground. The movement was so fast it was like everything skipped, like he was just there all of the sudden.

"I warned you, Gavin. Now I'll take back what's mine. You've shown me that you don't deserve my gift." Cernunnous lifted his staff with the glowing tip and Gavin began to change.

Shifting on his own was easy but when he was forced, the pain was intense and the change was bloody. His body jerked and folded in on itself as he fought to keep the creature free. He screamed and howled, tears streamed down his cheeks. In as many years as he had been alive, he only felt this one other time. No matter how many bruises, breaks, scrapes, gashes, or bite marks he received, this pain was infinitely worse then everything combined.

Cernunnous watched his Alpha change with a heavy heart. He picked Gavin originally because of his ability to shift at will, not by the lunar cycle. Unfortunately he did not know it came with a price.

The creature would take over and leave all reason behind. It would do what it wanted without a thought to the consequences. As long it was happy, nothing mattered. He found out that the creature did not just hunt to survive; it hunted for revenge. It had the skill of the wolf with the emotions of a human. Cernunnous had unwittingly unleashed an unstoppable fury on the planet.

At that moment, he took responsibility for what he had done, fixed the mistake he made all those years ago.

Gavin was on the ground, tears streamed down his face. Blood covered his shoulders and his knees. His heart raced so fast, it could be seen beating in the middle of his chest. It looked as if it could explode right out of his ribs. Each nerve stood on end and erupted into goose bumps all over his entire body, like thousands of tiny needles poked his skin. He moved to stand up and cried out in pain. Slowly he sat up. His chest heaved as he tried to regain his composure. "It burns like a fire in my lungs," he growled. He coughed a few times and then looked up to the god who now stood in front of him. "How dare you. You don't control me anymore. You lost that right long ago."

Cernunnous sighed. "I'm too late. You're too far gone. I'd hoped that there was still a semblance of a human mind left but I suppose that was gone long ago." He shook his head somberly as he turned to address Kal. "My child, come to me." He motioned to his side.

Kal stood up and walked forward slowly. The closer he moved, the warmer he felt until the warmth had washed away all the fear he felt. His skin prickled with excitement and his lungs filled with the heat. His body felt relaxed and at home. He began to feel the way he did all those years ago when pack meant everything and they would not even consider killing their own.

"You've done well taking care of my children. In all these years, you've helped them to survive. You protected them when I could not." He reached out a hand, the ivy stretched out to touch Kal. "I'm greatly saddened by the events that have transpired recently, whether in my name or not. His actions are my actions, but now, I must remedy the situation. Kal," he took the man's hand in his and grasped it as a sign of a pact. "You have been chosen." The ivy crawled down his arm and up Kal's until his forearm was entirely wrapped. "As my new Alpha, you will continue to serve me, protect the pack, and be my right hand. You will lead them under my rule as you have for so many years."

Gavin growled. "No! You chose him? He hid from the world when I would've taken control of this wretched planet." He pushed himself up with a grunt. "I have more strength than he'll ever have. I could lead better than he ever will. This is my pack and you won't take them from me!" he yelled. "You will not take what's rightfully mine! Not after everything I've done to get here." He lunged at Kal in spite of the agony his body felt. "It's all mine!" he howled.

Just before they connected, Kal fell to the ground with a grunt. His body cushioned Haydeez as she landed on top of him. She screamed in pain, her arm throbbed in protest. She had just enough time to look up and see Gavin over her, fury burned in his eyes.

He clenched his fist. Under the fur, his muscles bunched. "Do you think that'll stop me? I wanted to kill you all along. Besides, we had a challenge that hasn't been fulfilled yet. Pack rules say nobody else can interfere. And now you die," he growled. With his hand raised, he leaned back and yelled.

Before he could even move, his scream caught in his throat. Blood bubbled up and spilled out of his open mouth. It ran down his chin and dripped onto the grass. A look of surprise and fear crossed his face. He turned his pleading eyes to Cernunnous.

"I told you I had to take back what was mine. You were never immortal before I met you, Gavin. That was my gift to you as my Alpha. I couldn't let the leader of my pack die. But now, you've chosen your path and it appears to end here, tonight, by a hand other than my own," he said gravely. He nodded behind Gavin and everyone turned to look.

With one last shove, Linx used all of his weight and forced his knife as far as possible into Gavin's back. Warm blood poured out of the wound and raced down his back in a dark river. It bubbled out as tiny air pockets escaped to the surface. He moved to look into Gavin's eyes. "You know I never really liked rules. Couldn't understand them. I usually just do what I want," he said with a crooked smile. However, in Linx's eyes pulsed a rage so pure that even Gavin could understand what had just happened. "I almost lost someone very important to me and I intend to make sure you never have the chance to try it again." He leaned in close to Gavin's ear and whispered, "Guess this actually makes me your Omega. By the way, that's your lungs filling up with blood. Feels great doesn't it, you bastard."

He pushed him to the side and Gavin crumbled to ground. The last of his life trickled out of him as his body grew colder every second. Linx turned to Haydeez who was still face down on Kal where she landed. "Oi, already replacing me, love?" He glanced at Kal and noticed how completely nude the other man was and raised an eyebrow. "You realize he's in the nip right?" He looked at her arm and flinched. "We've got to get you somewhere to fix that before you lose any more blood." His heart was calm but he felt his cheeks flush slightly as he looked into her eyes.

Haydeez had used up what little strength she had left to shove Kal to the ground. She looked up at Linx, a crooked smile on her lips. Her words slurred as she spoke. "What took you? I had to do all the dirty work and you come in at the last minute to save the day, huh? Punk," she giggled. "Who's making all those little colored spots in the sky?" she asked as her head lolled to the side.

Kal moved her so she was on the ground and not spread awkwardly across his legs. He looked around for anything to cover up as his nudity seemed to make the humans uncomfortable. The ivy that had wrapped around his forearm spread out and grew up his arm, down his chest and covered his groin. He turned back to Haydeez to check her for other injuries.

She looked over at him and said, "Cool trick. How'd you manage that one?"

"I wish I knew," he answered, more confused than anything. He had never seen the former Alpha do anything like that before.

"I can answer that, Kal. The ivy is a gift. As my new Alpha you receive certain protections, benefits as you may call them. You can't be killed and you can heal your pack quicker than they can heal themselves. But the ivy is my thank you for everything you've done for them all these long years. You've stayed loyal, vigilant, and protected them the way an alpha should." He turned his gaze to Haydeez. "You've done more tonight than I could've thought possible of a female. We used to disregard your kind because they were weaker, poor fighters, and couldn't handle the dangers that would fall upon them in a war. You've shown me not to discount females anymore." The pack gathered around, some changed back to human form. "The children can stay. From this day forward I will no longer exclude females from my family. However," he said as his voice boomed across the island. "Should you take a human mate, I ask that you choose wisely. They must understand what they're entering into before you seal your union."

He looked down at Kal again and said, "Please pick her up, Alpha."

Kal nodded. He lifted Haydeez off the ground easily, his muscles barely took notice of the extra weight. Her head rested against his bare chest. He carried her over to Cernunnous with Linx at his heels.

Cernunnous put his hand beneath her chin and lifted her face so he could see into her eyes. "You are pack now, Haydeez. You have a place with us. No matter what, you can never be turned away and your safety is ensured among us." As he spoke, a tendril of ivy caressed her wounds. The blood flow slowed and the split in her lip closed.

Her eyes began to clear and she could move her fingers without pain. She blinked a few times and then looked down at her arm. The ache was gone and her nerves had stopped shrieking in agony. She touched her chest with her palm and felt her heart happily beat again at its normal resting pace. A dull pink scar was all that remained of the claw marks that had almost taken her arm off.

She looked up to meet Cernunnous's gaze and said, "Thank you. I'm not sure if I deserve the honor but I'll gladly accept it. You can never have too many allies." She glanced between Kal and Cernunnous and added, "Is it ok if I stand on my own now?"

The god nodded and said, "Of course."

She placed her hand on Kal's chest as he bent to set her back on the ground. The ivy touched her fingertips and flowed over the back of her hand as if to leave a gentle kiss. She smiled sweetly as her feet touched the ground. "You're a bit bigger than I remember. Alpha suits you." Her cheeks turned pink as she added, "Sorry for landing on you like that." She took a step back and heard someone behind her.

Linx cleared his throat. "By the way, you're welcome, love," he said sarcastically. "Can you walk?" He picked up her arm with his free hand and touched the scar. "Wow that was open just a few minutes ago." He shivered and shook his head. "Right. What do we do now?" he asked as he looked around at everyone.

Haydeez walked over to Gavin. She bent down and pulled Linx's blade from his back. After she wiped it off on the grass, she handed it to Linx and said with a smirk, "You may want to keep this around." She grabbed his arm, looked him in the eyes and added, "Thank you."

His chest got tight and his cheeks flushed. "Of course, love. Anytime." His voice was barely above a whisper. He cleared his throat and smiled awkwardly. "Told you you'd need me."

Cernunnous turned to Linx and motioned for him to come over. "Pack law says that you were wrong for interfering in a fight when an Alpha's challenged." He paused. "But you're not pack, and neither was he. I can't punish you for a rule you didn't break. However, I do feel that I owe you something for dispatching him as quickly as possible." He reached out his hand and took Linx's injured arm. The ivy touched his skin and caressed it the way it had done with Haydeez. After a soft hum and the rustle of leaves, the ivy retreated. "I know you didn't sustain those tonight but she cares for you and as such, we will watch over you as well. You, too, are under our protection."

Linx wiggled his fingers and flexed his hand. The muscles were warm. He swung his arm around and smiled. As he turned back to look at Cernunnous, he said, "Thanks, I didn't really do it for a reward or anything. It's just what I do." He turned to look at Haydeez and, with a sigh, he added, "I follow and protect."

Cernunnous walked among his pack. He greeted those in human form and gave a loving pat to those who remained in dog form. It was easy for Haydeez to see how much he loved them. In spite of his status as their god, he walked among them, talked to them, cared for them as a father figure. He loved them as if they actually were his own children. She understood why they continued to worship him long after his capture. They loved him just as much. For a god to take a personal interest in his subjects was amazing enough but he stepped out among them and physically touched each and every one, just to let them know he was there.

She watched them as she knelt beside Gavin. A thought crossed her mind that had her question if it was healthy that everything she had just been through was normal to her. She shook her head and looked down at the body. Gavin had been a young looking man who may have been considered attractive if his attitude did not get in the way but what she looked down at was something completely different. She called Linx over. "Doesn't this seem a little off to you?" she asked as she pointed at the body.

He looked down and said, "Who's the old man?"

"Gavin O'Connell, our psycho Alpha buddy. Remember that thing we found on Robley?" She rolled his body over and pointed to the brand. "Same symbol again. I mean, we knew he was released by Pandora but what the hell happened when he died? This whole thing is getting more confusing every day." She looked up at Linx.

He cocked his head to the side. "Looks like he aged really fast, like he had the life sucked out of him." He looked at Haydeez. "I bet it happened when the big guy took away his immortality. All the years hit at once." He shrugged. "We got the bad guy, love. Don't dwell on it."

Haydeez knew something was not right. She stared at the body for what seemed like forever. The only thing that brought her from her thoughts was when Linx grabbed her by the shoulder and shook her.

Chapter 32

The storm raged. Waves foamed all around the island. Thunder boomed and shook the ground on the shore. Lightning struck the land leaving a blackened patch of grass in its wake.

From his window, the old man continued his vigil. With his eyes on the island, he sighed. "Shouldn't be much longer," he whispered to himself.

He leaped up and ran for the phone as a loud boom echoed over the water and into his home. Before he could see anything outside, his fingers raced over the numbers on the phone. He felt an overwhelming heat for a moment and then everything went silent except for the ringing in the receiver. There was a voice.

"Something's happened. I don't know what but there be trouble for sure," he said frantically. He took a few tentative steps towards the window and looked out.

The storm had stopped completely and the waters beneath his dock were calm. The part that disturbed him more than anything else was what he saw when he looked out onto the island. Clear as day, he saw it. There was a small chapel with a candle burning in its tower. He shivered. "The spell be broken. The god is free," he whispered. The phone slipped from his hand and fell to the floor. He placed his hands on the window and watched.

He could see movement on the island as the bright light faded to a comforting pulse. There were dogs on the shore and the Alpha stood at the front of the pack. The woman was not visible but he could clearly see another man. He was incredibly tall with antlers on his head and an odd light emanated from him. There was no doubt as to who that man was.

There was a muffled voice in the distance but the old man paid no attention to it. He could not move his eyes from what he saw across the waters.

He had failed. The god was free and there was nothing he could do now. There would be a terrible punishment from the Council when they heard what happened. He did not want to think about what they would do. Slowly, he turned from the window and reached for the first sharp object he could find. He grabbed for a knife and ran his finger down the flat of the blade. There was nothing left for him.

A muffled voice called to him from across the room. It floated quietly from the receiver of his phone. He could not hear anything except for the sound of his steadily beating heart.

In a flash, he took the knife and slit his own throat. "I'm sorry brothers," he gurgled as blood poured from his throat and down his chest. He slumped onto the floor as the last bits of life spilled out all around his body. The only sound was the now angry voice on the other end of the phone that screamed for answers but received on silence.

•　　　•　　　•　　　•　　　•

"What happened? Are you there? What's going on?" Peter yelled. He slammed his fist on the thick oak table as the other Council members sat and watched. Peter was their contact with most of the outside sources. He handled all the calls and set up all the meetings.

He glared at one of the other men across the table, an older Slavic man with grey speckled throughout his hair and dark circles under his eyes. He looked older than his years, except for his eyes. The look he returned was filled with the same fire as Peter. "Is something troubling you?" he asked in a thick accent.

"Your people chose poorly," he said through gritted teeth. "The god is loose. Now we'll have him to contend with in addition to all the other trash left behind. Do you know what that'll do to us?"

"My Orthodox brothers didn't choose poorly. It appears that you have underestimated the value of your pawn," he answered. With his arms crossed over his chest, he leaned back in his chair and added, "It means nothing more now than it would if he'd remained trapped. We'll move forward as we always do." His voice held an air of disgust for the younger man.

He was about to make a comment when the Anglican representative spoke. "We're all in this for the same reasons. If we fight amongst ourselves, they've won. A single god for hundreds of other gods still trapped is an acceptable loss." He turned to the Slavic man. "Your brothers chose what they thought was best. Nobody could've predicted such an event as this one. His failure doesn't reflect in any way on the sincerity of your intentions on this council."

His eyes shifted to focus on Peter. "You're too quick to place blame. As the Catholic representative here, you need to learn patience and respect as taught by your priests. We've worked too hard at keeping in the shadows to allow something as trivial as this to cause a rift among us."

"My sincerest apologies, Venerated One," Peter said with a bow of his head. "My emotions got away from me. It won't happen again." His eyes flicked to the other man with a burning hatred. His blood boiled at the way he was treated. After all, Peter's people chose hunters who destroyed the opposition. The Orthodox man's people chose wizards to capture them and contain them with the knowledge that this day would come and now, it is here. He was disgusted and angry, but bit his tongue to keep the peace for now.

The Venerated One placed his hands on the table, his eyes drifted to each man. "Gentlemen, this isn't a problem. This is an opportunity. We must take this as a test of our faith in both our Council and our god. This was bound to happen one day. I'd hoped it wouldn't happen under the current Council, but it has and we're the ones to deal with it. We must pool our resources and regain control of the situation at all costs. Is that understood, gentlemen?"

They all nodded and responded, "Yes, Venerated One."

"Excellent. Then now's the time to devise our plan of action," he responded, relaxed and casual, as if they were discussing plans for Sunday afternoon tea.

Chapter 33

Haydeez raised her eyes to see where Linx was pointing. The first thing she noticed was that the storm stopped. Not only had it ended, but it looked as if it had not even happened at all. The waves subsided, the wind was calm, and she could see every star in the sky. Then she looked a little further.

Under the light of the full moon, on a hill on the shore of the main land, she saw it. Two people stood, hand in hand, and watched everything that happened on the island. Eyes squinted, she tried to see who it was even though in the back of her mind, she already knew. There was no mistaking it.

Pandora stood with her daddy. Patiently, she watched and waited for them notice her. With her pigtails and frilly black dress, she bounced on her toes in excitement. Haydeez grabbed Linx by the arm and pulled him down next to her. "Grab the bag and my shot gun. Let's get out of here now."

He nodded and ran off.

She stood up and moved towards the huddle of dogs and naked men and said, "Excuse me, Cernunnous? I think it's time for us to leave. I thank you for your kindness and for fixing what was broken," she lifted her arm, the shiny pink skin blended into the natural hue of her flesh. "But we need to go. We've got some other business to attend to tonight."

He extended his hand to her and said, "Haydeez, my new child, if you ever need anything, I'll do what I can to make it happen." He took her hand in his and the vines reached out to caress her skin again. "You're not the same as him are you? You're different. Are you a creature inside, like Gavin was with his two sides?" he asked, a hint of confusion on his face. He brushed aside the feeling and released her hand. "Travel safely, my child. Until we meet again."

"Pretty sure there's nothing else in there," she said with a chuckle. "Thank you again," she added. Her skin prickled where he touched her and her body felt warmer than it had when she had stood by herself. There was a certain calm that came over her whenever he touched her, like everything would be alright and he would take care of her. She shook her head and tried to clear her thoughts.

Linx walked up and bumped her on the shoulder. "Ready, love?"

She nodded her head and they walked down to the little row boat. All the while, the two figures remained motionless on top of the hill, bathed in moonlight.

•   •   •   •   •

Linx jumped out of the boat to tie it off, a renewed strength and vigor visible in every movement. He reached down and took the bag from Haydeez and then helped her out of the boat. They walked up the dock.

"Wonder where the old guy is now," Linx said as they walked past the little house. "Maybe he went to sleep," he said with a shrug.

"No time to stop and check," Haydeez said with a nod to Pandora. "We've got to deal with this right now."

The ground was wet but after the night they had, neither one of them cared about a little mud on their shoes. Dried blood plastered her clothes to her stomach and caused a chill to run through her blood. She had put her jacket back on and tried desperately to keep the air from reaching her skin. She kept her eyes on Pandora even though the child had not moved since the moment she saw her from the island.

"You're still alive!" Pandora said excitedly. She clapped her hands and bounced on her toes. "I wasn't sure who'd win but I'm so glad it's you. Did he hurt you a lot? I don't see any cuts or bruises or anything. Wow, you must've been really fast," she said, the childlike innocence returned to her voice.

Haydeez stopped and eyed the child. Something seemed different about her. She looked a little older but that was not possible. She could not just age like that. "I'm fine. What do you want, Pandora? I've got a lot of things to do," she said.

Pandora shook her head. "You're so impatient, Haydeez. You really need to slow down a little. You can't have everything all at once." She smiled sweetly. "I was watching you fight down there and I must say, you're pretty good. I can't wait until the next fight. I haven't decided yet what I want to give you but I'm sure it'll be really great." Her eyes sparkled as she spoke. She took great pleasure in not only the physical destruction of people but also the mental torture.

Haydeez eyed her cautiously. "What's wrong with you? You look different," she said. No sense playing games.

Pandora covered her mouth and giggled. "I'm growing up. Nobody stays a baby forever. I'm going to be a big girl soon." She glanced up at her daddy. "I can't wait to be a big girl again, like I was before I got trapped. Nobody should be trapped like that, Haydeez. Everyone should be free," she said, a slight twinge of urgency and sadness in her voice. It did not last long. "Have you found all my little friends yet?" A wicked grin spread across her delicate lips. "I don't think you have. You may have defeated the Loup Garou but you're not done yet. There's still so much more to do." She giggled again. Her eyes grew wide and she added, "Oh! I have to go." She looked at her daddy. "We have to plan. There's so much to do before we meet again."

Linx stood behind Haydeez with the bag over his shoulder and just listened. He was not about to have a repeat of the previous encounter. She already did not like him because he is a man. There was no reason to make her target him any further.

Haydeez was not sure what to do. Lately she had felt out of control way too often for her liking. She did not know how to stop Pandora yet but she did not want to let her go. She had to play the game the way Pandora wanted, but there had to be a way to know what was coming. "I hunt a lot of creatures. How will I know what's yours?" she asked.

Pandora giggled. "Silly Haydeez. If I tell you all my moves ahead of time, where's the fun? Just trust me when I say, you'll know." She looked back and forth between Haydeez and her daddy. With a heavy sigh that looked awkward on the child, she said, "Ok, I guess I can give you a hint, but just a little one."

Her eyes grew dark, shadows floated around in their blackened depths. Her voice was soft and enigmatic. "I'm sure you already know how to tell which ones are mine. All my babies are marked when I let them out. That way they know that I still control them." She paused, an eerie silence fell over the hill. Not even the sound of the water down below could be heard. Then she spoke in an unnatural voice reserved for the clinically insane in movies. "As the rivers flow to oblivion and the screams of the dead echo through the walls, you will know that the next level has been reached." The shadows in her eyes turned to thunderclouds and lightning flashed. "Three will become one and your end will be near, Haydeez. Choose now, heads or tails. You lose either way. We will see each other soon." The clouds disappeared as quickly as they materialized. Her face was child-like again and she bounced up and down with that same joy. "Until next time,

Haydeez." She waved vigorously like she was saying goodbye to a close friend.

Haydeez looked at her funny, an unsettling feeling in her chest. Goosebumps danced up and down her arms. She waved slowly like she was not really sure of what to do. The moments seemed to drag.

Then Pandora snapped her fingers and disappeared the same way she did in that field.

Haydeez turned to look at Linx and asked, "Did you understand any of that?"

Linx shook his head and said, "You mean did I understand any of the stuff the crazy little girl was saying to you? Oh sure. I understood all of it." He shifted the bag on his shoulder and added, "She's a bleedin nut. I can't believe we have to deal with her. She's absolutely gone."

"I really hope we can make sense of all this," she sighed. She wanted nothing more than to be able to stop Pandora. She never had a creature she could not defeat but this was not a creature. This was a creation, someone whose sole purpose is to destroy man. The weight of everything that had happened began to take its toll. Her body felt weak, her muscles ached, and her stomach growled like a lioness on the prowl.

"I know that look. We'll be fine, love." Linx squeezed her shoulder. "No worries, right?" He hugged her. "Let's get out of here."

Chapter 34

After a restless night, Haydeez and Linx packed their bags with the intent of heading back to Bristol where her plane patiently awaited their arrival. Plans do not always work out that way.

As they checked out at the front desk, a man in a suit walked up to them. "Excuse me, ma'am. Would you mind stepping over here for a moment?" He flashed a badge and motioned to a few chairs where a woman sat and watched them.

Haydeez raised an eyebrow and asked, "Did I do something wrong?" Her eyes fluttered and she smiled sweetly. She leaned her body against the counter and cocked her head to the side slightly.

"Ma'am, if you'll please just have a seat," he said, his voice low to avoid a scene.

She turned around and flashed a glowing smile. "Sure thing."

They walked over to the chairs and sat down. Haydeez and Linx placed their bags on the floor between their feet. The man held out his hand. The woman handed him a file folder. "I'm Agent Red. This is Agent Blue."

Linx covered his mouth in an attempt to hide a snicker. "Sorry," he said from behind his hand.

"And what can I do for you colorful agents this afternoon? Would you like some tea? Maybe some lunch?" Haydeez placed her hands in her lap and maintained her innocent persona.

Agent Red opened the folder and asked, "What business do you have in the British Isles, Miss Blackhawk?"

"All pleasure, Agent. Been doing a lot of sight-seeing. But, like any other vacation, this one has to end. Sadly, we have to be getting to the airport." She did a fake pout and then asked, "What agency did you say you were with?"

"We didn't," Agent Blue answered. "What did you see up here in Scotland, Miss Blackhawk?" She had an Irish lilt.

"We went to see the highlands. It really is a beautiful country, isn't it?" she said.

Agent Red looked up from the file. "Did you take any pictures, ma'am?"

"Unfortunately, I lost my camera in the water. I was standing on this amazing cliff when a big gust of wind came along and just took it right from my hands. Almost fell off the cliff myself, but cameras can be replaced. I can't." She looked at Linx and said, "We really should be going. Don't want to miss our flight."

The agents stood up together. "A lot of strange things have been happening over the last few weeks, Miss Blackhawk. Some of them have been incredibly dangerous," Agent Blue said.

"You might want to consider not coming back this way for a while, for your own safety of course," Agent Red added. "Wouldn't want you to get caught up in any of that and find yourself on the wrong side of a gun, ma'am."

Haydeez glanced at Linx and then back to the Agents. As she stood up a surprised look crossed her face and she said, "Well gosh, I do believe that I've just been threatened. Perhaps if you tell me what I did wrong, I might be more inclined to sit and talk but veiled threats and file folders I can't see really don't scare me. Now, if you agents will excuse me, my friend and I have a flight to catch. Since you know who I am, I'm sure you know how to find me. However, I can't be held accountable for anything that happens to you if you trespass on my property." She picked up her bag and added, "It's been a pleasure meeting both of you and I can already tell I'll see you again." She started to walk away but paused and turned around. "Maybe next time you'll have better manners. Hopefully, you'll learn that it's quite rude to threaten a lady." She felt a slight prickle on her arm as she brushed past Agent Red. Her skin felt warm and her nerves danced like she had been hit with static electricity. She ignored the feeling for the moment and walked out the door with Linx right behind her.

They got to the car and threw their bags in the trunk. Linx got in and started the car. He waited for Haydeez to close her door before he said, "So which agency do you think they're with?"

Haydeez bit her lip in thought and finally said, "Not sure. I'll have to check with some people to see what's out there but it's got to be something international. You don't usually have Russian agents operating on British soil."

Linx cocked an eyebrow. "How do you know one of them is Russian?" he asked.

Haydeez smiled. "Agent Red pronounced some of his words with a slight, almost unnoticeable accent. Yea, I'm that awesome," she said.

Linx laughed. "I see." He paused. "You think they might be from D.O.G.M.A.? I only worked in I.T. so I have no idea how they named the agents but anything is possible right?" he asked.

She stared out the window for a moment and saw the agents leave the hotel. Her fingers absently rubbed the part of her arm where she grazed the strange man. "I'll figure it out eventually. When I do, I'll be sure to let them know that I know who they are. They had the chance to be nice but that's all over now." She gave them an evil look and blew a kiss.

They pulled out of the parking lot and headed south to Bristol.

Haydeez could not shake the uncomfortable feeling she had from her encounter. Even the Alpha did not make her feel like this. It felt like bugs crawled under her skin. Her nerves were on edge and she shivered. "I don't like that they know who I am. I'm willing to bet they know your real name too," she said. "Something about them just isn't right. Maybe Joseph can explain it." She shivered again. "I really don't like this."

"It'll be fine, love. Honestly, what could they really do to us? If we absolutely needed the help, we've got an army for back-up now," he chuckled. "Not to mention you do pretty well for yourself all on your own."

She chuckled. "Pretty well? Yea I guess I do."

•   •   •   •   •

Haydeez and Linx sat at a large wooden table in a windowless room. They sipped coffee and waited. Exposed beams crossed the ceiling and the polished stone walls, a combination of decoration and support. Wall sconces cast dancing shadows with their flickering candles. There was very little other decoration in the room. It was simple but elegant.

A man walked through the archway off to the left. He held a tray of food. As he set it down on the table, he took a seat across from Haydeez. His face was a mixture of confusion and pride as he said, "So let me get this straight. You've uncovered a plot to destroy mankind, released a Celtic god, destroyed his Alpha who was also a Loup Garou, and managed to piss off an international organization that knows who you are. Did I miss anything?" He clasped his hands and placed them on the table in front of himself.

Haydeez cleared her throat and put her cup down. "Actually you missed the part where we became official members of Cernunnous's pack with all the perks and protection except immortality." She lifted her arm to show the new pink skin where she was healed. It now looked more like a scratch than the gash that had been there a few days before. By the looks of it, she probably would not even have a scar to show for her efforts.

He shook his head slowly and said, "Of course, how could I forget that?"

"Don't forget that you destroyed a religious building that came to life and started chasing you. Wish I'd seen that one," Linx chuckled. He grabbed a sandwich and put it up to his mouth to take a bite but stopped as he noticed he was being watched. "Sorry," he mumbled and took a bite.

"Look, Joseph, I did what I had to do to stop him. I had no idea that chapel was guarded by a golem and I definitely didn't know it would come to life when I took the piece," Haydeez said. "And now I've got this crazy little girl with Pandora stuck inside her who is stealing babies for a reason I have yet to discover, and she wants to play a game with me." She sighed. "It sounds absolutely ridiculous when I say it," she said as she started to laugh.

Joseph raised an eyebrow and exchanged a look with Linx. "You know, I always thought you got way too serious about these hunts. It's nice to see this." He motioned to her and leaned back in his chair. "Did you have enough to eat? I could make something else if you'd like. The only time I really bring anyone here is when they're completely unconscious and I need information. I don't really do much entertaining." He grabbed a cup and poured himself a drink.

Linx shook his head. "No I think we're ok," he said with a sideways look at Haydeez. "*Ok* being a relative term of course."

Haydeez shoved Linx as she tried to stop laughing. "Would you prefer I sit in the corner and cry? Everything just sounds even more absurd when you actually say it." She wiped a tear away. "I really don't know what I'm doing. I mean, she was created with the sole purpose of destroying *man*. She even said she had no intention of hurting me. She said that we immortals have to stick together or something. I have no idea what she was talking about. I'm not immortal." She chuckled again.

Joseph took a sip of his drink and stayed quiet. He had found Haydeez when she was just a baby and raised her as his own. He was the only father she knew and the best trainer she ever had. From a young age, she wanted to do what he did and so he encouraged it as long as she spent part of her time using her brain and the other building her muscles. They trained part of the day and studied the other part.

Until she became old enough to go out into the world on her own. She saw other people in relationships, with regular jobs, and decided the hunter's life was not for her anymore. She fought hard to get what she wanted but Joseph held firm. He told her she was above all the pettiness of the rest of the world. Her young mind did not want to believe him anymore. So she left in search of her normal life.

"It's been a long time since you've sat in a corner crying and I don't see you going back to it. As for you being immortal, she's just trying to get under your skin. Her whole purpose is to destroy. Why would she want you on her side?" Joseph asked. In the back of his mind, he held onto a secret. Once she found out, it would either destroy her or make her the most formidable foe anyone has ever encountered. But she was not ready yet. Someday she would be but not now. There was too much to focus on to drop this on her tonight. So he kept it inside and waited while it slowly ate away at his subconscious like a tiny leach trying to suck every ounce of blood from its victim. On the outside, he remained his normal thoughtful self.

They sat in silence for a moment until Haydeez, with a mouthful of food, said, "Oh! What about our colorful new friends?" She wiped a bit of food from her face as she said, "Sorry."

Joseph shook his head and said, "I'm not sure but I've narrowed it down. There's only so many international organizations that investigate paranormal or supernatural activity. Also, from what you've told me, they might have supernatural people on staff as well. I'll do a little more digging and let you know when I find something, but it sounds like Linx here might be right about them being from D.O.G.M.A." He took another sip and then placed his empty cup on the table. "So, what now?"

Haydeez and Linx looked at each other and both sighed.

"We wait, I suppose," Haydeez said. "For now, we have no idea what she's up to or what she'll release next. So unless you've got yourself a pretty little magic ball that tells the future, we're stuck."

"I can't believe you're still this pessimistic," Joseph said with a sigh. "Well, I'll see what else I can find out and give you a call. You haven't changed your number on me again, have you?" he asked sarcastically.

Haydeez looked down for a moment and said, "No, I learned my lesson last time." She looked up at him and added, "People learn." She stuck out her tongue.

He laughed and stood up. "Then I guess I'll call you when I find anything. It shouldn't be too long before you hear from me. Do you need me to show you out or do you remember the way?"

Linx and Haydeez stood up. She said, "I think I remember. If you find us wandering around down here tomorrow, you'll know we got lost... again." She chuckled.

He came around the table and hugged her tight. "You'll be fine. Everything will work itself out," he whispered in her ear. He paused for a moment and squeezed a little tighter as he added, "I'm proud of you." He pulled back and winked at her. "And stop bringing that boy to my home. I don't like him," he added loud enough for Linx to hear.

"I knew it!" Linx said as he stood up. Haydeez grabbed him by the arm and started to walk out of the room. "Let me know what you find," she said over her shoulder. She had to drag Linx along behind her.

They walked past several rooms with polished stone walls and exposed beams. Every room had a beautifully hand carved archway. There was one area that was blocked off with a plastic tarp. A collection of dirt peeked out from under the tarp as they walked past. "Wonder what he's putting in," Haydeez muttered casually. "Guess we'll see next time."

After a few minutes they reached a metal door with a heavy lock. She easily pulled it open and stepped out with Linx right behind her. The door closed with a click and the lock slid into place.

They made their way up into the house above. The upstairs was decorated in a mix of western and Native American. There were dream catchers in the windows and a steer skull above the front door. A beat up couch sat with its back against the window. In the kitchen, there was a small two-seat table, a chair, and a refrigerator that looked like it belonged back in the sixties.

The place looked like a dump. Anyone who snuck around would see the very ordinary, run down shack of a poor man. If they took the time to look, they might find the hidden door tucked away in the corner of the basement. If they managed to open the door and get inside they would find a secret hallway that led to a maze full of rooms with polished stone walls carved out of the earth itself. But it would be the last thing they saw. Anyone who walks those halls had better be invited or they would find themselves on the wrong end of whatever weapon caught the Blackhawk's fancy that day.

Chapter 35

Haydeez stood on the docks south of Ocean City in New Jersey. The wind rushed around her and tossed her hair in every direction. A storm was on its way in and she did not want it to mess up her drive home. She leaned against the side of her jeep, arms crossed, and tapped her foot. The only thing on her mind was how long it would take to get on the road and if she could beat the sleet.

A car pulled up with its headlights turned off. It stopped and the engine quieted. A man in a business suit stepped out of the passenger side door and smoothed down his coat. He reached into the car, pulled out a brown leather briefcase, and quickly closed the door behind him to trap the heat inside. He walked up to Haydeez with the smile of a car salesman and said, "So lovely to see you again." He had a New York tongue and smelled of cigars.

"You're late," she said as she shouldered herself off the jeep and reached for the case. "All of it better be there."

"Of course, darling. Have we ever not kept our end of the deal? And I've been informed that there will be more travelers this evening." The words slid off his tongue like a snake. He leaned to the side and looked into the jeep over her shoulder. His smile widened. "Five vacationers. We've made room for everyone. So there's no need to worry." He handed her the case and waited patiently as she examined the contents like she always did.

The wind made it difficult to check the money but Haydeez used her body as a shield and did the best she could. When she was satisfied she said, "I hope you brought the light like I suggested. Otherwise, it'll be an incredibly bumpy ride. They have to stay solid until you get to... Where did you say you were headed?" she asked.

He placed his hands behind his back and said, "I didn't but nice try. Kudos to you for the effort."

She shrugged and closed the case. "Never hurts to ask." She set the case on the front seat and locked the door. Then she motioned for him to walk with her around the back to gather the statues.

She unzipped her back window and began to pull them out one at a time.

"Hurry, you've only got a minute before they're not solid anymore."

He turned and walked quickly to the trunk of the car. The driver had stepped out and opened the trunk already. He was waiting with a UV light of his own, It shined brightly in spite of the hour of night. They had mounted it to the trunk to avoid the possibility of the bulb being crushed by one of the little stone creatures.

They transferred all the statues to the trunk without incident. She zipped up her back window and said sarcastically, "A pleasure as always. Be sure to give Peter a great big kiss from me."

The man looked at her funny and opened his car door. "We'll be in touch," he said before he slid into the warm, plush comfort of his car. He closed the door and the engine purred to life. They drove off and left Haydeez alone in the cold.

"Wow, I'm hungry," she said to herself. "Still there, Linx?" she asked.

"Always. Everything alright, love?"

"Not sure, but I'm not about to sit out here on this frozen dock pondering life's little mysteries. I'm grabbing some food and then I'll be on my way," she climbed into her jeep and turned the key. It broke the silence as it protested the cold and finally started. "Time to go home, baby," she whispered.

"We'll be here when you get back," Linx said.

"Who's we?"

"Me and Bebo."

"Bebo isn't allowed in the house, Linx. He's being punished. He tried to eat the seat on my motorcycle."

"But he's cold and lonely. Plus, he asked so nicely."

"Linx, put him in the barn."

"But he looks so comfy by the fire."

"Linx."

"Sorry, I can't hear you anymore."

"Linx!"

"I'll see you tomorrow, love."

"Linx!" she yelled but he had already hung up. Something between a growl and a groan escaped her lips as she left the docks in search of an all-night fast food stop. She was excited to finally head home after everything that had happened recently. She thought to herself that she might actually get a few minutes to breathe and relax. In the back of her mind, she called herself an idiot to even consider such a silly notion.

Epilogue

Haydeez sat by her fireplace and drank a cup of hot chocolate with more marshmallows than necessary, through a swirly straw. With her feet up on the couch and her head on the arm rest, she tried to make sense of everything. There was just too much that had happened that she did not understand and she did not like it.

For weeks, she had racked her brain in a useless attempt to figure out what Pandora's next move was. She had gone over what the child said again and again but still could not figure out what was next.

Linx picked up her feet and flopped down on the couch. "If you don't stop thinking about it, I'm going to get you so pissed that you'll pass out and actually get some real sleep. To figure this out, you'd have to be as cold and single minded as she is." He propped her feet up on his knees. "Relax."

She groaned. "I can't. Every time I try, my mind wanders and I end up thinking about all this garbage again." She took a sip. "Pandora's out there somewhere with her plan already in motion and I'm just sitting here drinking cocoa and laying on the couch."

They sat in silence for a long time. They listened to the fire crackle and enjoyed the quiet of each other's company. Haydeez was so relaxed that she actually started to doze off. Then, a noise broke the silence like a glass that shattered on the floor.

Haydeez jumped and almost fell to the floor as she reached for her phone. When she looked at the number she said, "Hmm, it's my favorite mystery man." She pressed the button to answer. "Hello, Peter. What can I do for you this lovely November evening?"

"We have a job for you, Haydeez. You're not busy are you?" he asked sarcastically.

"Just taking a nap but I'm never too busy for you," she responded in kind. With a glance at Linx, she rolled her eyes. "What do you have for me this time?"

Note from the Author

Word-of-mouth is crucial for any author to succeed. If you enjoyed the book, please leave a review online—anywhere you are able. Even if it's just a sentence or two. It would make all the difference and would be very much appreciated.

Thanks!
Rebecca

About the Author

Rebecca Flynn has always been interested in different mythologies. After her husband introduced her to her favorite author, she became inspired to write her first book. With her debut novel, *The Wild Hunted*, leading the way, she hopes to continue telling the stories of the main character, Haydeez Blackhawk. She currently lives on top of a mountain in Rockwood, Tennessee, with her husband, 4 children, and her pack of 7 dogs.

Thank you so much for reading one of our
Supernatural Fantasy novels.

If you enjoyed our book, please check out our recommended title for
your next great read!

The Graveyard Girl and the Boneyard Boy by Martin Matthews

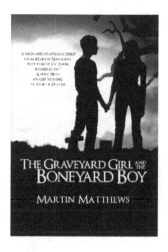

"... a compelling and eminently likable cast of characters." –*Authors Reading*

View other Black Rose Writing titles at
www.blackrosewriting.com/books and use promo code
PRINT to receive a **20% discount** when purchasing.

CPSIA information can be obtained
at www.ICGtesting.com
Printed in the USA
LVHW092017291219
641989LV00002B/193/P

9 781684 333592